FRIENDLY

PET FRIENDLY

Sue Pethick

KENSINGTON BOOKS
www.kensingtonbooks.com

KENSINGTON BOOKS are published by

Kensington Publishing Corp.
119 West 40th Street
New York, NY 10018

All Kensington titles, imprints, and distributed lines are available at special quantity discounts for bulk purchases for sales promotion, premiums, fundraising, educational, or institutional use.

Special book excerpts or customized printings can also be created to fit specific needs. For details, write or phone the office of the Kensington Sales Manager: Kensington Publishing Corp., 119 West 40th Street, New York, NY 10018. Attn. Sales Department. Phone: 1-800-221-2647.

Kensington and the K logo Reg. U.S. Pat. & TM Off.

eISBN-13: 978-1-61773-843-2
eISBN-10: 1-61773-843-3
First Kensington Electronic Edition: January 2016

ISBN-13: 978-1-61773-842-5
ISBN-10: 1-61773-842-5
First Kensington Trade Paperback Printing: January 2016

10 9 8 7 6 5 4 3 2 1

Printed in the United States of America

To Willie, the best darned dog a girl ever had

Acknowledgments

Many thanks to my agent, Doug Grad, for recommending me for this project; to my editor, Gary Goldstein, for trusting me to complete it; and to Elizabeth May, for making it better without bruising my ego. Hugs and gratitude also to the family and friends who kept me sane and cheered me on through this process; to my daughter, Lindsay, who staggers me with her wit; and to my wonderful husband and biggest fan, Christopher Pethick. Where would I be without you?

CHAPTER 1

It was odd seeing a dog at a man's funeral, Todd thought as he glanced at the little mutt sitting in the pew, but that was Uncle Bertie for you—odd. The dog's name was Archie and he was the fourth dog with that name that Todd's uncle had owned over the years, every one of them a well-trained part of Bertie's stage act.

Todd's mother liked to say that her brother was the only person she'd ever known who actually carried out his threat to run away and join the circus. Uncle Bertie had spent three decades touring the world, and when living out of a trunk became too much for him, he'd begun a second career performing at kids' birthday parties and volunteering at nursing homes. In his handwritten will, he'd asked that there be no tears at his funeral.

On the other side of the pew sat Todd's sister, Claire. She'd flown in to help their mother clean out Uncle Bertie's apartment and make arrangements for the funeral, and she'd be leaving after the reception. Claire had been in a snit ever since their mother agreed to give Archie to Todd, and he didn't want her to leave town if there were any hard feelings.

He nudged her with his knee.

"You mad at me?"

She shook her head. "But I still think you're making a mistake. Gwen's never going to let you keep him."

"Will you cut it out? She's always saying she wants a dog someday."

"Someday, sure, but not today and not a dog like that, either."

"What's wrong with him?"

Todd looked down at the little fur ball lolling in the pew beside him and smiled. Archie had a mass of unruly white fur and a patch of tan that looked like the faded remains of a black eye, but there was a warmth about him that was as comforting as a hug. Todd reached out and patted him protectively.

"Nothing," Claire said. "But I'll bet he's not the pedigreed pooch Miss Gwendolyn Ashworth had in mind."

Todd ignored the barb. If his sister thought Gwen was a snob, there was nothing he could do about it. He decided to change the subject.

"Did the boys get my present?"

She rolled her eyes.

"Yes, and it's driving me crazy. Did you have to do *all* the dogs' voices?"

Todd had sent his nephews a prerelease sequel to his megahit game app, Pop Up Pups, and he'd been anxious to find out what they thought. Claire's eight-year-old twins were his most reliable product testers.

"So they like it?"

Claire couldn't suppress a smile.

"Of course they like it. Their friends think they've got the world's coolest uncle."

Todd grinned. "No argument there."

"I thought Gwen was coming," Claire said.

"She was," he told her. "Something came up at work."

"You pop the question yet?"

He shook his head.

"But you're going to."

"Of course."

Claire nodded tactfully, but Todd knew he'd be getting an earful later. She glanced back at the rest of the mourners.

"So, what do you think?"

He smirked. "What a bunch of clowns."

It was true. With the exception of the immediate family, every person sitting behind them had come in greasepaint to honor Bertie Concannon, a man who'd been clowning longer than many of them had been alive. Though barely five-six, he'd always seemed larger than life. He had an Irishman's gift of gab, a voice that could fill a theater clear up to the cheap seats, and hair a shade of orange unknown in the natural world. Uncle Bertie had never had much, but he never seemed to need much, either. He was funny and carefree and utterly ridiculous, and Todd had admired the hell out of him.

The service began and the mourners stood for the first song. As the opening strains of "Just a Closer Walk with Thee" rose from the pipe organ, Archie sat up and looked around. He cocked his head and whimpered; his chin quivered and his eyes grew misty. Then, as the organ music swelled, the little dog began to howl.

Claire's comment continued to weigh on Todd's mind at the reception. As he passed through the crowd, accepting condolences and offering homemade *hors d'oeuvres,* he wondered if adopting Archie was a mistake. His relationship with Gwen was serious—serious enough that Todd was planning to propose to her that weekend—but they'd been living together for only a few months and there'd already been a few bumps in the road. Would adding a pet at this point really be a good idea?

A succession of clowns was coaxing Archie to do the tricks that he and Uncle Bertie had used in their act. As Todd watched the little dog dance, play leapfrog, and give high fives, he felt his anxiety start to lessen. He'd spent the last five months creating virtual dogs for his game app; it was going to be fun having a real live dog again. And once Gwen met Archie, he told himself, she was going to love the little guy too.

A clown in a pink wig sidled up and took a crab cake from his tray.

"So, you're Bertie's nephew," she said. "What is it you do?"

Todd hesitated. The success of Pop Up Pups had been a pleasant surprise, but he wasn't comfortable with the public attention it had brought him. The billion-dollar acquisition of his previous start-up hadn't garnered any interest outside the business world, but thanks to his game app, he was on the verge of becoming a household name.

"I write game apps for smartphones," he said.

"Anything I might have heard of? My kids play a lot of those."

She popped the crab cake into her exaggerated mouth.

"Ever heard of Pop Up Pups?"

She swallowed. "That's *you?*"

He nodded.

"Wow. My kids would play that game all day if I let them."

A hobo clown with a pile of cheese puffs on his plate gave Todd a curious look.

"Hey, I know that game. Isn't one of the pups named Archie?"

"That's right." Todd smiled. "It was sort of a tribute to Uncle Bertie."

Inspired, he said a few words in the virtual Archie's voice, a sound *GamePro* magazine had described as "a Rottweiler on helium."

"Right," the hobo said, his eyes narrowing. "You do the voices of the dogs, too. I think I read something about that."

"So," the pink-haired clown said as she shifted the last two crab cakes onto her plate. "I hear you're adopting Houdini."

Todd frowned. "Who?"

"Houdini." She pointed at Archie, whose ball-balancing act was getting cheers from the guests. "Bertie's dog."

"You mean Archie?"

"I guess." She shrugged and brought another crab cake to her mouth. "But Houdini's the only thing Bertie ever called him."

When the last guest had departed, Archie was passed out under the coffee table. Todd took the trash out to the Dumpster and headed back inside. Claire and their mother, Fran, were in the kitchen, cleaning up.

"It was a good service," Fran said. "Nice reception, too. Bertie would have liked it."

Claire slipped on a pair of rubber gloves and started washing the serving dishes.

"A few of them cried, though," she said. "Bad form."

Todd popped an olive into his mouth and grabbed a dish towel.

"They were sad clowns. That doesn't count."

"Too bad Gwen couldn't come," his mother said. "Another big project at work?"

"Mmm. Something like that."

"Well, I suppose work comes first," she said. "You know what they say: 'The difference between ordinary and extraordinary is that little extra.'"

"Right," Claire said. "And hard work never killed anyone, but why take the chance?"

Fran took out a stack of Tupperware containers and began lining them up on the sideboard.

"Are you sure you want to take Archie?" she asked Todd. "Claire says there's room for him on the plane."

"I'm sure," he said, setting the turkey platter back in the cupboard. "And even if I wasn't, there's no room for a dog on one of those little puddle-jumpers."

"But you and Gwen just got settled. Don't you think it'd be better not to add another complication?"

Claire was scraping the last of the Jell-O mold into the sink. "Give it a rest, Ma."

Todd gave his sister a grateful smile. He loved his mother, but it was hard to get her off a subject once she got started.

Fran was indignant. "Why? What did I do?"

"You're butting in."

"Who's butting in? I just think it's the considerate thing to do, especially if he wants to marry this girl."

Todd shot Claire a dangerous look. "Who says we're getting married?"

"Oh, don't blame your sister," Fran said. "Anyone could see you're crazy about Gwen, and why not? A girl like that doesn't come along every day."

"I agree," he said. "But I'd still appreciate it if you'd let me handle this my own way."

"Well, I suppose you know best," Fran said, looking doubtful.

"I do," Todd said, kissing her cheek. "And don't worry. Gwen'll be thrilled."

Archie was quiet on the way to the airport. As the car inched its way through traffic, he lay on the backseat, shifting his gaze between the two people in front. Todd watched him in the rearview mirror.

"I think Archie misses Uncle Bertie."

Claire glanced back over her shoulder.

"What makes you think that?"

"I don't know. He just looks kind of sad."

"He's probably just carsick. Bob says dogs don't really have feelings like we do."

Todd held his tongue. Bob was all right as a brother-in-law—he was a good provider and he loved Claire and the boys—but he had a habit of stating his opinions as facts, and God help you if you disagreed with him. If his sister wanted to believe that Archie had forgotten Uncle Bertie, that was fine, but Todd knew a sad face when he saw one.

Claire opened her purse and started rifling its contents.

"So, why didn't you call Gwen?"

"I didn't want to bother her at work," he said.

"There's still time to change your mind, you know."

He shook his head. "No, thanks."

As he waited for the cars around them to start moving again, Todd's mind began to wander. In a little over forty-eight hours, he'd be asking Gwen to marry him. If she said yes, he thought, he'd be the happiest man on earth. If she turned him down . . .

"I see you've bought your girl a ring."

He jumped. It was like his sister had been reading his mind.

"How'd you guess?"

"You've had your hand in your pocket all day, Todd. I just *hoped* it was a ring you were holding." She held out her hand. "Can I have a look?"

He took the velvet box from his pants pocket and passed it over. Claire snapped the lid open and gasped.

"Holy moly! Where'd you get this, Buckingham Palace?"

She took the ring out and watched it catch the light.

"Gwen saw it in a jeweler's window a couple of months ago," Todd said. "I'm going to pop the question this weekend."

He stuck out his hand. "Now, give it back."

Claire kept the ring just out of reach.

"Not so fast. I haven't had a good look yet."

Todd's embarrassment turned to pride as he watched his sister's reaction.

"You like it?"

"Of course I like it," she said. "But, Todd, it must have cost a fortune."

He shrugged. "Not quite."

She put the ring back in its box and handed it over.

"Are you sure about this?"

"Why, you think she's too good for me?"

"No, I think you're too good for *her*." Claire tapped her forehead. "You've got a *brain*. All she does is gossip about people she doesn't know and prattle on about the stuff she owns or wants to buy."

Todd felt his lips tighten. "How can you say that? You've only met her once."

"Once was enough. I don't know what you see in her, but I certainly know what she sees in you."

Todd pretended he hadn't heard. If Claire thought that Gwen cared only about his money, there was nothing he could do to change her mind.

"Sorry," she said. "I know it's none of my business. I just don't understand the attraction. There was a time when you would have seen right through a girl like that."

There it was, Todd thought. The unspoken accusation that he suspected Claire had been holding against him for years. When was she going to let it go?

"This is about Emma, isn't it?"

She crossed her arms and looked away. "Not necessarily."

"When are you going to get it through that thick noggin of yours?" He reached over and tapped her temple playfully. "That girl doesn't exist anymore."

Claire's eyes flashed. "How would you know?"

Todd felt a stab of guilt. Things had happened back then that his sister wasn't privy to, but if she was going to blame him for something he didn't do, he figured she should at least know the truth.

"Maybe I should have written to her," he said, "but when Dad died, things changed. I had to get a job. Then there was the house to take care of, and you and Ma. I don't remember hearing any complaints about that."

Todd swallowed the lump in his throat. Looking back, it felt as if losing his father had cut his life in two. He understood why it had happened, knew he hadn't been the only one forced to adjust to a new reality, but he resented it when Claire accused him of being heartless.

Claire's voice softened. "I know that, *dearthái.*"

"And don't go all Irish on me," he snapped. "Emma's home life was a mess; things were never going to work out between us. Ma said it'd be better if I didn't write to her, so I didn't. End of story."

"I'm sorry," she whispered. "I didn't know."

"It was a long time ago," he said, gripping the steering wheel tighter. "I've got a good life now. The last thing I need is to be pining for Emma Carlisle."

He heard the scream of jet engines; Archie dove for cover as the 747 passed overhead. Todd reached around the seat and patted the little dog's head.

"It's okay, boy," he said, grateful to be changing the subject. "That's just how civilized people fly: with reclining seats and restrooms and tiny bottles of booze."

Claire craned her neck, taking note of the bumper-to-bumper traffic that jammed the Interstate in all directions.

"Oh, yeah. This place is real civilized." She took out her ticket. "Terminal D, smart guy."

They pulled up to the curb and Todd grabbed his sister's luggage. As he closed the hatchback, a cold blast of air nearly knocked him over. He set her bag down on the sidewalk.

"You want help with this?"

"I'll be fine." Claire's hair was buffeting her face. "But you'd better roll up that window. Feels like a storm's moving in."

Todd glanced back at his car. Sure enough, one of the back windows was open.

"Thanks for telling me," he said. "I didn't realize I'd left that down."

They hugged briefly.

"Call me when you get home," he told her.

Claire grabbed her bag and smiled. "Call me when Gwen says no to the dog."

"She won't," he said. "But thanks."

"I'll talk to you later," she said. "And, Todd? Good luck."

Todd waited until Claire had disappeared into the crowd before getting back into the car. Archie was sitting up in back, an expectant look on his face.

"How you doing back there?"

The little dog tipped his head and whimpered.

"Must have been cold back there with the window down.

You want to move up here?" He patted the passenger's seat. "Be my guest."

As Archie settled down on the seat beside him, Todd started the car. Claire was wrong, he thought. Gwen was going to love Uncle Bertie's dog just as much as he did.

CHAPTER 2

Emma Carlisle was not having a good day. In fact, at that very moment she couldn't remember the last time she'd actually had a good one. When she inherited the Spirit Inn from her grandmother, she'd thought her life was finally turning around, that all the lousy relationships, rotten jobs, and just plain bad luck in her life had been payment in advance for her once-in-a-lifetime windfall. Instead, it seemed as if karma was once again having a big ole laugh at her expense. *You thought you were out of the woods?* she heard it snickering. *Ha-ha! Fooled you again.*

This latest bout of karmic deserts was being served up by Harold Grader, her up-until-now friendly local banker, who'd apparently decided that loaning her more money to maintain and upgrade her hotel would be throwing good money after bad.

"I'm sorry, Emma," he said, looking anything but. "The committee just isn't going to approve another loan when you're only making the minimum payments on the one you have."

"I understand," Emma said, "and I know it doesn't look good, but business has really been picking up."

"Yes, I can see that," he said, prodding the financial statements on his desk with the tip of his finger. "But your overhead has also increased. If anything, it looks as if you're making less on a per-guest basis than you were before."

Emma closed her eyes in silent acknowledgment. It didn't make sense to her, either, but she'd been over the figures a dozen times and every time it came out the same. It was as if her profits were vanishing into thin air.

Maybe I'm just incompetent.

No doubt that's what her banker was thinking. Emma had worked at her grandmother's inn every summer since she was six and could do any job on the property, yet when people heard that it had been gifted to her, they just assumed she was a neophyte, a manager in name only who left the real work to her older, more experienced staff.

It didn't help, of course, that Emma didn't look like the kind of businesswoman a bank was used to dealing with. She was a little below average height; her figure was more boyish than buxom; and she considered makeup to be a waste of both time and money. She liked the convenience of shorter hair, but had grown hers out after being mistaken once too often for a preteen boy. At work, she wore a suit and the highest heels she could walk in without breaking an ankle, but her days off were spent in T-shirts and jeans.

Grader was fiddling with his pen. "What does Mr. Fairholm think of your proposed changes?"

Emma tried not to resent the question. Clifton Fairholm had been her grandmother's assistant manager since the Spirit Inn opened, and Gran's will had stipulated that he be allowed to keep his job when ownership of the hotel changed hands. He was as stumped by the inn's problems as she was, but his fondest memories were of the hotel in its heyday, and convincing him to modernize the place was like forcing a fish to fly.

"I'd say he's on board with most of them," she said.

"Most, but not all?"

Emma chewed her lip. She'd only said "most" because she wanted her answer to sound plausible. The truth was, Clifton Fairholm didn't think much of any of the changes she was proposing. But then, she thought, her assistant manager probably wouldn't agree to add indoor plumbing if there'd been a choice.

"Well, you know Clifton." She chuckled. "Always a stickler for historical accuracy. Anything new puts his knickers in a twist."

Grader pursed his lips. "So, he's had some objections?"

"A few. Yeah."

She squirmed. *Don't ask, don't ask, don't ask.*

"May I ask which ones?"

Emma sighed. If she hadn't been so desperate, she'd have gathered up her financial statements, told Grader what he and his committee could do with their money, and walked out. As it was, however, she didn't think she could stay in business much longer without it. If she didn't turn things around soon, she'd be forced to sell the Spirit Inn to pay her creditors. It'd be like losing Gran all over again.

"What about the coffee bar?" Grader prompted.

She realized that she'd dug her fingernails into the arms of the chair and released her grip. *Relax,* Emma told herself. There were good reasons behind every penny she was asking for. Grader was only doing his job. This wasn't personal; it was just business.

"He thinks it's unnecessary," she said. "He says we already serve coffee in the restaurant."

Grader considered that. "Does he have a point?"

"Yes, but people like coffee bars. Having to go into the restaurant, wait for a table, and then sit down to order is a hassle when all you want is a latte while you read a book."

The banker's face was impassive. "Anything else?"

She took a deep breath. "The automated key cards. Clifton

thinks they'll 'diminish the historic ambience' of the inn," she said, making air quotes with her still-stiff fingers.

"Won't they?"

Emma frowned. She'd have thought that improving the hotel's security was a no-brainer. Was Grader just trying to be difficult?

"Did they have key cards in the nineteenth century?" she said. "No, but people want to know their stuff is safe when they leave their rooms. Plus, guests steal our keys all the time."

Grader seemed taken aback. "Surely not."

"Okay, maybe *steal* isn't the right word. Let's just say that a significant percentage of our guests leave without returning their keys, which means that before I can rent the room again I have to get a locksmith to come out, replace the lock, and make new keys for everyone on staff."

"You could charge the guest for that."

"I could," she said, feeling her temper rise. "But I'd have to spend a lot of time on the phone listening to them complain about it, and in the end we'd probably lose the chance to have them back. Believe me, the costs are significant."

"More than an automated system?"

Emma was losing patience. She'd gone in there with a simple business proposal. Why the inquisition?

"Obviously not," she said, "but there are some things that our guests want and need that can't be *amortized*."

She saw heads turning her way and shrank back.

"Sorry."

"That's all right," he said. "I know you feel strongly about this, but a well-run hotel shouldn't have to borrow to cover its overhead, and there's no guarantee that any of the changes you're proposing will improve your financial position. Unless and until the Spirit Inn can show a profit, I don't see how we can give you another infusion of cash. It's just too much of a risk."

Emma looked down, refusing to concede defeat. So what if Grader turned her down? There were other banks out there. She didn't care how long it took; she would not take no for an answer. The Spirit Inn meant too much to her to give up now.

She started gathering the papers from the loan officer's desk.

"Thank you for your time," she said, placing them back in the Pee-Chee folder that served as her briefcase. "I guess I'll just have to find the money somewhere else."

Grader shifted in his seat and stared at the pen he was twirling in his fingers.

"Look, maybe I could run your request by the committee again."

Emma's heart leaped; she could have kissed him. Instead, she gave a dignified nod.

"Thank you. I appreciate it," she said, handing him the Pee-Chee folder.

"Don't thank me yet," he said. "To be honest, I doubt it'll make any difference."

"It doesn't matter," Emma said. "Just the fact that you're willing to ask means a lot."

Grader waved away the compliment and set the folder aside.

"I admire your spirit," he said. "But I think you're making a mistake. You're a young woman. Why hang on to a white elephant like that? You could sell it, take the money, and see the world. If she were still alive, I think your grandmother would agree."

"I know that," Emma said. "But I don't want to see any more of the world than I've got right here. I know that sounds crazy, but it's true."

"All right." Grader sighed and shook his head. "But don't say I didn't warn you."

He walked her to the door and they shook hands.

"I'll submit your request tonight and call you when the loan committee makes its decision."

As the door closed behind her, Emma almost wilted with relief. Maybe things hadn't gone as well as she'd hoped, but at least he hadn't said no. Harold Grader was probably just making sure that she knew what she was doing. Why else would he have asked her all those questions? He was a banker, after all. Bankers were supposed to be careful with their money. If he didn't think the committee would approve her loan, he wouldn't have agreed to run it by them.

The more she thought about it, the surer Emma was that her loan would be approved. She could pay off her bills, give herself some breathing room, and start moving the Spirit Inn squarely into the twenty-first century. And after that, she thought as she got back into her truck, there'd be no stopping her.

Emma was halfway home when the first drops of rain hit her windshield. As she started up the winding road that led to the Spirit Inn, she congratulated herself for having put the studded tires on her truck the day before. Down in the valleys, they could wait until November to prepare for winter, but up here even a moderate amount of precipitation could quickly turn to ice, making the roads hazardous.

The inn her grandmother had left her was situated on a large plat in the middle of an evergreen forest. Ski resorts and newly minted tech millionaires had been snapping up the land around her fifteen hundred acres, but Emma refused to sell. To her, the towering trees were like the spires of a natural cathedral, the ferns and wake-robin as ethereal as stained glass.

I've got to find a way to save this place.

The box of supplies lurched from one side of the cab to the other as her truck continued up the hill. Emma was anxious to talk to Clifton about her meeting with Grader and hoped he wouldn't be upset that her plans were still alive. After all, she told herself, his reluctance had nothing to do with her. Some people just had a hard time with change.

As her truck rounded the last curve, the road widened and Emma smiled. The inn's parking lot had filled in the time she'd been gone and people were gathered on the front porch, laughing and hugging the new arrivals as they hurried to escape the rain.

This would be the sixth time that the SSSPA had held their annual convention at the Spirit Inn and Emma saw several people she recognized from years past. A few of them spotted her truck and waved as she drove by. She smiled and returned their greetings, grateful for their loyalty. They were a well-behaved bunch who paid their bills and were easy on the furnishings, she thought. Who cared if they were a little strange?

Emma pulled into a parking space marked *Reserved* and hauled the box of supplies around to the inn's back entrance. Two small steps led to a concrete landing just outside the back door. Emma balanced her box on the cast-iron railing and fished the key out of her pocket. In the past, the back door had always been left unlocked, but since the inn's financial difficulties had begun, she'd had to ask the staff to be more conscious of who had access to the supplies. She didn't accuse anyone, and had no evidence even if she'd wanted to, but in the last few months both she and Clifton had noticed a sharp uptick in the restaurant's overhead. If someone had been helping themselves to the pantry, they needed to stop.

When the supplies had been safely put away, Emma walked down the path to her private quarters, a tiny cottage her grandmother had built shortly after buying the inn. She took a quick shower and donned her "uniform," the green blazer, white shirt, and green-and-gold ascot she wore to work. The tie had been Clifton's idea, ascots having been popular back when the inn was built, and her grandmother insisted it be standard attire for everyone on staff. Emma's black pencil skirt, which she wore instead of slacks, was one of only two things that distinguished her from the rest of her staff, the second being something else that Gran had insisted upon: a name tag that said *Emma Carlisle—Manager*. She ran a comb through her hair and headed back up the path to the inn.

The lobby was a hive of activity. Recent arrivals, still damp from their trip through the parking lot, stood in line at the front desk, anxious for a chance to freshen up after hours on the road, while those who'd checked in earlier milled about, looking for familiar faces and discussing the weekend's upcoming events. The bellboys were in constant motion, loading their brass carts and whisking them away before scurrying back like dandified Energizer bunnies.

At the front desk, Clifton Fairholm was projecting his usual air of unruffled efficiency, his movements as deft as a croupier's, but the new clerk, Adam, seemed harried. When Emma asked discreetly if there was anything she could do to help, the young man gave her a look of such gratitude that her heart went out to him. She suspected that Clifton, whose standards were as high as his patience was short, had been pushing the young man hard. When this rush was over, she'd have to speak with him about it.

When the line had been dealt with and the inflow of new arrivals had slowed to a trickle, Emma went out to visit her guests. The first-timers were usually satisfied with a brief hello, but repeat customers expected to be given a few minutes to talk about previous visits and fill her in on what had been going on in their lives since they'd been there last. Clifton had never understood her enthusiasm for the meet and greet, referring to it as "politicking," but Emma found it the most enjoyable part of her job. What was the point of owning a hotel if you didn't like people?

She was halfway across the lobby when the sound of tinkling bells alerted Emma to the approach of Viv Van Vandevander. Viv was in her late sixties, a full-figured woman with wavy salt-and-pepper hair that fell from a middle part to just past her shoulders. Her typical outfit was a version of what Emma thought of as hippie chic—peasant blouses and voluminous skirts in deeply saturated colors—and her signature sound came from the talismanic *suzu* bells sewn onto her velvet slippers. According to Viv, the ringing of the *suzu* bestowed positive power and authority to their possessor, while at the same time warding off evil spirits. An asset, no doubt, in Viv's line of work.

"Emma, dear, how are you?"

The older woman embraced her briefly, then studied her at arm's length.

"Your aura is very blue tonight."

Emma was always at a loss when Viv made one of her pronouncements.

"Uh, thanks?"

"However"—Viv frowned—"I see smudges of brown in the background, which are disturbing. Have you been troubled lately by distracting or materialistic thoughts?"

"Well, now that you mention it—"

The older woman clasped her hands together. "I knew it!"

"Knew what?" a hearty voice boomed.

Emma turned and saw Viv's husband, Lars Van Vandevander, approaching with a beverage bottle in each hand. Lars was a professor of parapsychology and the organizer of that year's SSSPA conference.

"They don't carry Kombucha," he said, handing a bottle to his wife. "I'm afraid you'll have to make do with Snapple." He smiled at Emma. "Nice to see you again, my dear."

Viv took a sip of her drink and continued her diagnosis.

"I was just telling Emma that she must free herself from her attachment to the material if she's to have any hope of clearing her aura."

Lars nodded and took a sip of his Trop-a-Rocka tea. "Mmm."

"If you embrace the things that are true and worthy in the world," Viv said, staring deeply into Emma's eyes, "whatever vexations you face will melt away."

Emma doubted it would be much help with the loan committee, but she thanked Viv for the advice.

"I see Dr. Richards is here," she said, pointing to an awkward-looking man standing by the fireplace.

Dick Richards was Lars's rival for the leadership of the SSSPA's local chapter, and the two men spent a large portion of every conference trying to win converts to their latest pet theories. Emma didn't know or care much about their research, but she preferred Lars's friendly, easygoing personality to the prickly, obsessive Richards, whose pointed nose and snow-white hair made him look like an irritated egret.

"Oh, yes," Lars said. "Dick's got himself another new theory this year. It should be fun helping him disprove it."

Viv swatted him playfully.

Emma glanced around. "Has Dee arrived yet?"

The other two exchanged a troubled look.

"She's here," Viv began. "But . . ."

"Dee isn't well," her husband said. "I fear this may be her last conference."

The news was sad, but not surprising. Dee was one of the older members of the Van Vandevanders' group, and Emma knew her health had been failing. Dee and her grandmother had been great friends, and when Gran passed away, Dee had transferred her affections to Emma. Sharing each other's company had been like a salve on the wound left by their mutual loss. Now Emma felt hot tears pricking her eyes.

"What's wrong, do you know?"

"Her heart, most likely," Viv muttered. "I told her years ago—"

"Perhaps she should tell you herself," Lars said. "Dee's always been a very private person."

"Of course," Emma said. "I won't tell her you mentioned it."

Emma made her excuses and walked off to continue welcoming the other guests, trying not to let the thought of dying make her feel weepy. It seemed wrong, somehow, for all the vitality that a human life contained to just disappear. She believed in heaven, but it still depressed her when someone she cared for died. Maybe that was why she was willing to put aside her skepticism for a few days every year when the SSSPA showed up. If it made losing someone less painful, she thought, why not believe in ghosts?

CHAPTER 3

Claire's doubts about Gwen and Archie continued to echo in Todd's mind after he'd dropped her off, and by the time he took the freeway exit toward home, his confidence was shaken. Yes, he and Gwen had talked about getting a dog someday, but it was also true that neither of them had said what kind of dog they wanted or how soon "someday" might be. And if Archie wasn't the dog she wanted, or "someday" wasn't now, what was he going to do?

The more Todd thought about it, the more annoyed he was with his little sister. Why did she have to think the worst of Gwen? He hadn't been at all worried about adopting Archie until she planted all those doubts in his head.

It didn't help that his proposal was planned for that weekend, either. Todd had been knocking himself out trying to make sure that everything would be perfect on Sunday: dinner at Gwen's favorite restaurant, champagne and red roses at the table, the ring. No matter how many times Gwen said she loved him, there was always a voice inside Todd's head telling him it couldn't be true, that someone as desirable as Gwendolyn Ashworth would never want to be with him for the long run. If only she would say yes on Sunday, Todd thought, he could finally stop doubting that his happiness would last.

As if sensing Todd's unease, Archie reached out and put a comforting paw on his leg. Todd looked down at him and smiled.

"What do you think? Should we pick up some dinner on the way home? Maybe grab a pint of Ben & Jerry's while we're at it?"

Archie sat back and pawed the air happily.

"I'm glad you agree," Todd said. "What woman could say no to a pint of Cherry Garcia?"

As he returned to the car with his groceries, Todd felt a renewed sense of optimism. Of course Gwen would forgive him, he thought. Once she met Archie, she'd be as nuts about the little fluff ball as he was.

"Wait'll you see what I got for you," Todd told Archie as he loaded the bags in back. "A dog bed, a chew bone, and a bag of the most expensive dry food on the shelf."

He set the bags inside, closed the hatchback, and slid into the driver's seat. Archie was watching him intently.

"Okay, when we get home, I'll set the table and put dinner in the oven while you check out the backyard. Then, when Gwen gets there, you can come in and meet her. What do you think?"

Archie barked once as his tail went wild.

"I'm sure she'll be happy to meet you, too."

Todd pulled slowly into the driveway and killed the Volvo's engine. Gwen's car was already in the garage.

"Hmm," he said. "She must have come home early."

Archie's head drooped.

"No, don't worry. It's going to be fine. Just let me think a second."

Walking through the door with a dog in his arms would be a bad idea, he thought. As good-natured as Archie was, he still represented a big change in their lifestyle, and Gwen deserved to have a chance to talk about any misgivings she had before meeting him. Once she was comfortable with the idea of its being "the three of them," Todd would make the introductions.

"Okay, change of plans," he said, grabbing the door handle. "Stay here. I'll be right back."

The house was quiet when he stepped inside. Gwen's coat was in the closet and her purse was on the kitchen floor next to her shoes, but the TV was off and there was no sound coming from the back bedroom. Todd paused at the bottom of the stairs.

"Anybody home?"

He heard a scuffling sound overhead and the rapid click of high heels. Then Gwen appeared, wearing a black lace dress and a pair of pink stilettos. Her long blond hair had been pulled back in a chignon, revealing the sapphire-and-diamond earrings Todd had given her for Christmas, and there was a mischievous twinkle in her blue eyes. When she saw him at the bottom of the stairs, she threw her arms wide.

"Well, what do you think?"

Todd stared up at her, agog. "Wow. You look amazing!"

"I'm glad you approve," she purred, descending the stairs.

"I do." He kissed her. "But why the fashion show?"

"Oh, I don't know," she said. "Maybe it's because I'm *taking you out!*"

She grabbed his arms and shook them excitedly.

Todd felt his smile falter. "Tonight?"

"Of course tonight." She laughed. "Look at you. You'd think somebody *died*."

Gwen's hands flew to her face.

"Oh, my gosh, I am so *stupid*. You just came from Bertie's funeral." She took his hand and led him to the living room. "I just got so excited about taking you out that I completely forgot."

Todd ran a hand through his hair, wondering what to do. There was no way they could go out and leave Archie alone. Since losing Bertie a week ago, he'd been bounced from the kennel to the funeral, and then there'd been all the strangers at the reception to deal with. What the poor dog needed more than anything was a quiet place where he could feel at home with people who loved him. Todd just hoped that Gwen would understand.

"Can I get you something?" she said. "You want a drink?"

"No." He shook his head. "I'm okay. It's just—"

"How was the funeral? Were there a lot of people there?"

He nodded, stalling for time. Todd hated giving people bad news, especially when they were likely to be as disappointed as Gwen would be. Maybe he could just tell her he was too tired to go out.

"It was fine," he said. "A lot of his friends from the circus came."

"Not too depressing, then. That's good."

She stood and did a slow turn in front of him.

"So, what do you think of the dress? Pretty hot, huh? It's a Nicole Miller—"

"What about dinner?"

Gwen stopped mid sentence and frowned.

"We're going out, remember?"

"Oh, yeah." He nodded. "Right."

This was not going well.

"Todd, what on earth is the matter? Did something bad happen at the funeral?" She shook her head. "You know what I mean."

He slumped forward. "I feel like an idiot."

Gwen gave him a strained smile.

"I'm sorry, sweetheart, but you're not making sense."

"I know." He sighed. "The thing is, I bought dinner on the way home—one of those roast chickens they sell at Safeway. I'm sorry."

"Oh. Well, that's okay. We can go clubbing after." She looked around. "Where is it?"

"In the car."

With the dog!

"Hold on a second. I'll be right back."

Todd sprinted out the door and down the front steps. It was going to be all right, he told himself. Archie hadn't been out there long, and the chicken was in one of those plastic things that you practically needed the Jaws of Life to pry open. Maybe Archie wasn't even hungry. After the day he'd had, the poor dog had probably just passed out on the front seat.

But when he turned the corner and saw the Volvo, Todd's heart sank.

The car's windows, foggy from chicken heat and dog breath, were streaked with greasy paw prints; the remains of a shopping bag hung limply over the backseat; and on the dashboard, Todd could just make out the mangled bottom of the chicken container. Archie, however, was nowhere in sight.

He heard footsteps approaching from behind.

"Hold on," Gwen said, trying to catch up. "I can't run in these shoes."

Todd's voice was hoarse. "Archie."

"Bertie's dog? I thought he died."

"He did," he said, still staring at the car. "I meant the new one."

"What's he got to do with our dinner?"

Todd felt a surge of hope; Gwen still hadn't noticed the car. He wheeled around, trying to block her view of the Volvo.

"Nothing. He was at the funeral. He sat in the pew with us."

He could feel sweat breaking out like a rash all over his body. Any second now, Gwen was going to notice the greasy paw prints on the car windows and all hell was going to break loose.

"Aww, I'll bet that was cute," she said.

"It was. And at the reception, he did a bunch of tricks that Bertie'd taught him."

This was torture, Todd thought. Why hadn't he just called and told her he was bringing Archie home?

"I love it when dogs do tricks," Gwen said. "Hunter and Nikki have a papillon that walks on her hind legs and it's soooo adorable."

"Yeah, well, Archie can do a lot more than that."

"Really? Oh, I'm sorry I missed it."

A slow smile spread across Todd's face. Maybe things weren't so bad after all. If clever tricks were enough to win Gwen's affections, it would be no problem at all convincing her to keep Archie.

"I can show you, if you'd like."

Gwen shook her head. "Maybe later. The food's probably getting cold."

"I don't mean a video. I mean live. You know, in person."

Her face fell. "What are you saying?"

He'd been hoping for a better introduction, but there was nothing he could do about it now. Besides, Gwen could hardly blame Archie for making a mess of the car. It was Todd's fault for leaving him in there with the food. He took a deep breath and swallowed hard.

"Mom promised Bertie that the family would take care of Archie, and I told her that we'd been talking about getting a dog. . . ."

Gwen's eyes narrowed. "Uh-huh."

"Of course, I knew I should talk to you about it first. . . ." He winced.

"Oh. Why didn't you say that before?" Gwen looked around, confused. "And what's that got to do with—"

As her gaze settled on the Volvo, her eyes widened.

"It's okay," Todd said, lunging for the car. "Don't worry, I'll clean it up."

He grabbed the rear door handle and yanked. Archie was on the floor, crouched over the remains of the chicken carcass. Fat dripped from his muzzle, and the clear dome of the container was perched on his head like an oversized helmet. Todd chuckled nervously.

"Gwen, meet Archie. Archie, this is Gwen."

She cleared her throat. "Hello, Archie."

The little dog stood, his tail between his legs, and took a shaky step forward.

"Poor guy," Todd said. "I didn't realize he was so hungry." Gwen's face was stony. "Clearly."

"Still, it's not a complete disaster. I bought dessert, too."

As if on cue, Archie staggered from the car and vomited onto the driveway. Gwen stared at the mess on the ground.

"Let me guess," she said. "Cherry Garcia?"

"What were you *thinking?*" Gwen snarled, throwing her Jimmy Choos into the closet. "That you could just waltz in here with that *mutt* and I'd be happy about it?"

Todd was sitting on the bed watching her get ready for bed. They'd been arguing for hours and he could feel his resolve weakening. Every time he thought that things were settled and Archie would be allowed to stay, Gwen rekindled the argument and he'd find himself apologizing all over again. He felt like a prizefighter being pummeled against the ropes.

"I thought we agreed to give him a chance."

"Right," she snapped. "Like I had any choice in the matter. What was I supposed to say? 'No, Todd, you may not keep a dog in your own house'?"

"It's not my house; it's *our* house."

"Of course it's *your* house," Gwen said, her voice catching. "I moved in with you, didn't I? Honestly, sometimes I think you don't realize how much of an outsider I feel like around here."

"I thought that's why we redecorated. So you could feel like the place was yours, too."

She hung up her dress. "Yes, and now you hate it."

"I don't *hate* it," he said. "It's just taking a while for me to get used to the changes—that's all. And what's that got to do with keeping Archie?"

She took off her earrings and dropped them into her jewelry box.

"Forget it. You wouldn't understand."

Gwen slammed the closet door and stomped off into the bathroom.

Todd lay back and stared at the ceiling. He couldn't see any way to end this fight except to admit defeat and get rid of Archie. Gwen was right. He should have asked her before taking the dog, and he certainly should have known better than to leave Archie in the car with their dinner, but that didn't mean he wasn't pretty peeved about the way things were turning out.

The comment about the house was especially galling, considering that he'd spent almost a hundred thousand dollars to make it "hers." At the time, Todd told himself it was an investment in their future, that if Gwen wanted to feel more comfortable there, it meant that she could see herself living with him permanently. His married friends were always saying, "Happy wife, happy life," but what about his happiness?

Oh, stop being such a baby.

So he had to get rid of the dog, he thought. What was the big deal? It wasn't as if he and Archie had a long history together. Todd had seen his uncle's dog maybe three or four times before the funeral, and most of those were when he was performing with Uncle Bertie. Whether the little guy ended up with Todd or his sister probably didn't make much difference to him one way or the other. The only one who'd really be affected was Todd.

The phone rang and Todd glanced at the clock. As he reached for the receiver, he checked the caller ID. It wasn't a number he recognized.

"Hello?"

"Mr. Dwyer?"

"Yes."

"This is Beth Johnston, your neighbor across the street. We met at the block party last year."

"Oh. Hi, Beth. What's up?"

"I hate to be calling so late, but I thought you should know that your dog's over here."

"I don't have a dog," Todd said. "I mean, I do, sort of, but he's in the garage."

"Well, your garage door is open and I know for a fact that he's been running around the neighborhood for at least an hour. My kids were playing with him for a while, but they've gone to bed now and I'd like him to go home."

Todd looked out the window. How had the garage door gotten open?

"I'm sorry, Beth. I'm sure it was closed when I put him out there."

"Yeah, well, I don't want to be a grouch, but there are leash laws, you know."

"No, no. I understand. I'll come right over and get him."

He put the phone down and knocked on the bathroom door.

"That was one of the neighbors," he said. "She says Archie's in her yard."

The door flew open. Gwen was standing there in her night-gown.

"How did he get out?"

"Apparently our garage door's open. I'm going to go get him. I'll be right back."

Todd marched downstairs, wondering how the automatic garage door could have been opened. He hoped it wasn't some kid playing a prank—or worse. No wonder Archie had been so quiet, he thought. The little scamp hadn't even been inside. He grabbed a jacket off the hook and headed out the front door.

Archie was sitting on the sidewalk in front of the John-stons' house, staring longingly at an upstairs window where two small faces peered down from between parted curtains. As Todd started across the street, he waved at the window. The faces disappeared and the curtains closed.

He took Archie home and set him on his new bed, stroking the little dog gently as he settled in for the night.

"There you go," he said. "Snug as a bug in a rug."

Archie nuzzled his hand and sighed contentedly. Todd felt a pang. He should have called first. If he hadn't rushed things, maybe Gwen wouldn't have gotten so upset. But now?

"We'll see how it goes in the morning," he said. "No mat-ter what happens, though, I promise you'll have a good home."

Todd stood and headed back inside, pausing at the thresh-old to disable the garage door opener. He still couldn't figure out what had happened; without one of the remote controls, a person would have to press the button on the inside panel to open the garage door. He frowned thoughtfully and glanced back at the small dog snuggled comfortably on his bed. The button was more than four feet off the ground. Was it possible . . . ?

Todd shook his head and walked back into the house.

Houdini indeed.

CHAPTER 4

With the first night's banquet successfully concluded, Emma headed back to her office, exhausted but pleased. The menu from her chef, Jean-Paul, had gotten raves from the SSSPA, and the presentation had gone off without a hitch. Once she cleared the paperwork off her desk, she could go back to her quarters for some much-needed sleep.

Adam was checking in a late arrival at the front desk and the bellboys were having a lighthearted argument about who should take the man's bags. Emma guessed that the teens' friendly competition meant they'd already made more in tips that day than either one had expected. Nevertheless, she doubted the windfall would last them more than twenty-four hours. As she approached, the bantering stopped and the boys greeted her with flirtatious smiles. She stepped behind the front counter and shook her head, bemused.

I might be single, she thought, *but I'm not that desperate.*

"Mr. Fairholm's in your office," Adam said. "He said he needs to discuss something with you before you leave."

Emma's gut tightened, but she kept the smile on her face.

"Thanks. I'll go see what he wants."

These end-of-the-week "discussions" were getting to be a

habit with her assistant manager. Instead of bringing his concerns to her as they came up, Clifton would wait and spring them on her all at once—generally at a time when Emma was too tired to come up with a satisfactory response. Tonight's discussion was bound to be more troublesome than usual, too, as she'd also have to tell him about the bank's reconsideration of her loan. She hoped, however, that the changes she'd been working on would satisfy at least some of his objections and get them back on the same side again.

Clifton was sitting in the chair behind her desk. When Emma walked in, he jumped to his feet, but she motioned him back down, taking one of the visitors' chairs for herself. She slipped off her shoes and began rubbing a cramp out of her instep.

"It's been a madhouse around here today," she said. "Thank you for taking care of things."

"No thanks needed," he said. "It's my job."

She nodded. Clifton had never been one to accept compliments graciously.

"Adam said you have something you need to discuss with me, but before we get to that, I thought you'd like to know that Harold Grader agreed to resubmit my application to the loan committee."

Clifton pursed his lips. "I'm sure you're pleased."

Emma took a second to consider what she was going to say next. Like it or not, she and Clifton were stuck with each other. She had a moral obligation to honor her grandmother's wishes, and at his age, he'd be hard-pressed to find another job. He knew more about the inn and the way it worked than she did, and they both knew it, but doing things the way they always had been—his way, in other words—was driving her out of business. If they were going to save the Spirit Inn, she and Clifton would have to work together.

"I thought about what you said regarding the coffee bar," she said, "and I think I have a solution. What if we put it where the store is now? We wouldn't lose any square footage in the lobby that way, and the renovation costs would be minimal."

He shook his head.

"We can't eliminate the store. Our guests appreciate the convenience."

"Well, then, what if we kept the most-requested items behind the front desk and listed them in the room directories? When guests need something, they could buy it from one of the clerks."

Clifton's nostrils flared. He probably found the thought of handling their most-requested items—toothbrushes, deodorant, and foot powder—unappetizing.

Emma set down her right foot and started massaging the left one.

"Of course," she said, "it would mean more work for the front desk staff. I'd understand if you don't think they could handle it."

It was a calculated move on her part. Clifton considered the front office his personal fiefdom, and any suggestion that his clerks might be unable to cope would have to be vigorously refuted.

"Not an issue," he said. "My staff is fully capable of doing whatever is required."

"Hmm, if you're sure," she said, smiling sweetly.

Clifton narrowed his eyes, looking even more than ever like a silent movie villain. Poor man, Emma thought. With his carefully parted, brilliantined hair and pencil-thin mustache, he really did seem to be from another era. He wasn't married, and as far as she knew he didn't have any friends, either. What on earth did a guy like that do on his days off? Nothing outdoors, judging from his pasty-white skin. Of course, he never offered any information, and she never asked, either. Emma figured that as long as her employees showed up on time and did their jobs, they didn't owe her an explanation for anything they did that wasn't illegal. She'd had enough trouble in her own life to make her not want to go prying into the affairs of others.

"Have you had a chance to ask about the missing restaurant supplies?" he said.

"It's on my to-do list," she said. "I figured Jean-Paul had enough on his mind with the banquet tonight."

Clifton had been harping for months on the discrepancy between the amount of food being purchased by the chef and the number of diners he was serving, but Emma wasn't convinced that the difference was great enough to risk upsetting the man. Jean-Paul was a talented chef, and he was willing to work for much less than he was worth. Even if he was wasting some of their staples, anyone she hired to replace him would cost her more than whatever she'd paid for them.

He took a deep breath and gave her a pained look.

"It's not my decision, of course, but are you sure you're not being naive with regards to Jean-Paul? With his history . . ."

"He paid his debt to society, Cliff. Unless he does something to make me think he's relapsed, that's all I need to know."

The subject of Jean-Paul's drug conviction was a sore point with Emma. Her mother's struggles with drugs and alcohol had shown her how hard it was for ex-addicts to move back into the mainstream and how quickly they became dispirited when they felt that no one would give them a second chance. Jean-Paul had been sober for more than a year when she hired him, and his weekly drug tests proved that he was no longer using. In spite of Clifton's doubts, when it came to drug abusers, she was anything but naive.

"Nevertheless," he said, "there have been discrepancies."

Emma's hands started shaking. She balled them into fists.

"I don't know why we're losing money, but I do know that Jean-Paul isn't the problem. Or at any rate," she added, "he's not the whole problem."

"I didn't say he was." Clifton seemed offended. "I merely suggested that we consider all possible explanations."

Emma's anger vanished in a cloud of self-doubt, and with it the last of her energy. She nodded.

"Don't worry," she said. "There are still plenty of places we can cut costs. Once the bank comes through with the money, we'll be fine."

When Clifton had gone, Emma trudged back down to her cottage and collapsed on the sofa. She'd been feeling pretty good until their meeting. Now she felt weary to her bones. She looked around at the tidy, empty space and felt tears start to well up. *I've been surrounded by people all day,* she thought. *So why do I feel so alone?*

Emma reached for a tissue and blew her nose. It wasn't the first time she'd asked herself that question; the fact was, she'd felt lonely for most of her life. Her father had died when she was only three, too young to have formed more than a vague impression of a man with large hands and impossibly strong arms, and the rest of her childhood was spent pretty much on her own, her mother being too strung out most of the time to care. Summers with her grandmother had saved her from stumbling down the same path, but even that time was spent mostly in solitary pursuits: Running the inn didn't leave Gran much time to do stuff that kids enjoyed. Once in a while a family with kids would stay at the inn, and for a little while Emma would have a companion or two, but there were none she'd ever really thought of as friends.

A smile played across her lips. Well, she thought, there was one exception: the Dwyers.

Todd and Claire Dwyer. Boy, she hadn't thought about them for ages. Todd had been a year older than Emma, Claire a year younger, and when the Dwyers came to the inn, they were like the Three Musketeers—one for all and all for one. The three of them spent their days exploring the woods and the nights lying on the cool grass, watching for shooting stars. Emma got her kicks making fun of the "city kids," but they were pretty cool about it. She taught them how to build forts and climb trees and they showed her what it was like to be part of a normal family. Todd had even given Emma her first kiss.

She blushed, remembering what a disaster that had been. It was an innocent gesture, but she'd been pretty well-defended back then, and without even thinking, she'd punched him in the stomach. To cover her embarrassment, she told him that he would have to give her fair warning the next time.

It had taken two years for Todd to try again, and as she recalled, there'd been no punching that time. When he left that summer, they'd vowed to stay in touch, but it wasn't to be. Todd never wrote to her, and the Dwyers never came back to the Spirit Inn.

As Emma's life had continued its downward spiral, Todd became a symbol of the sort of love and stability she longed for. While her mother partied and argued with her druggie friends, Emma would hole up in the bedroom and fill the pages of her theme books, writing, *Emma Dwyer, Emma Dwyer, Emma Dwyer.*

CHAPTER 5

No one slept well that night. Archie, locked in a strange garage, spent hours howling in protest while Todd threatened, cajoled, and begged him to be quiet, and Gwen, furious at the situation, lay in bed in wakeful, sullen silence. By the time Todd got out of bed, he'd given up on his plan to keep the little dog. He got dressed and went downstairs to call Claire.

"Just don't say I told you so," he said when she answered the phone.

"You know I won't," she told him. "I'm just sorry for your sake that it didn't work out."

"Yeah, me too."

"You could give it a few more days. She might change her mind."

"No." Todd heard whimpering coming from the garage and lowered his voice. "Gwen'll just be looking for an excuse to get rid of him and I'll go crazy trying to keep him out of trouble. It wouldn't be fair to any of us."

"So how do you want to do this?" she said.

"I thought we'd bring him out to your place today, if it's all right. If we hurry and get on the road, we can make it there by five."

"What about your proposal?"

"The reservations are for tomorrow night. We'll be back by then."

"You're going to be dead tired after all that driving. Why not ask her next weekend instead?"

"No, thanks, I'm anxious enough as it is."

"Well, the boys will be thrilled to see you. Can you guys stay the night? We've got plenty of room if you don't mind sleeping on the pullout."

Todd hesitated. A sleeper sofa was fine with him, but he doubted Gwen would feel the same. Anything less than the Four Seasons was the same as roughing it, as far as she was concerned.

"I'll let you know," he said.

Claire's voice had a hard edge to it. "Not sure it's good enough for Her Highness?"

"Please don't make this worse," Todd said. "I feel bad enough as it is."

"You're right," she said. "That wasn't fair. If you need to just drop him off and run, that's fine."

He closed his eyes gratefully. "Thanks, sis. You're the best."

Claire laughed.

"You just figured that out, did you?"

Todd set the phone down and steeled himself before going out to the garage. After the ruckus Archie had raised the night before, he was prepared to find a mess on the floor and the dog bed in tatters. Poor Archie. He'd lost Bertie and been stuck at the kennel all week with a bunch of strangers; now he was going to be cooped up in a car all day.

When Todd opened the door, though, he was pleasantly surprised. Not only was the floor clean and the dog bed intact, but Archie was waiting patiently, his tail beating a happy cadence on the concrete.

"Hey there, buddy. You doing okay?"

Todd bent down to pet him and the little dog leaped into his arms, covering his face in dog kisses. As he held the squirming ball of fur that nuzzled him with a wet nose, tears sprang to Todd's eyes. Why couldn't Archie have been like this last night? If only Gwen had seen what a sweet guy he really was, she would never have wanted to get rid of him. Now that her mind was made up, though, the only thing for Todd to do was to get Archie to his forever home as quickly as possible. As he set the little dog back down, he consoled himself with the thought that someday, he and Gwen would have a dog they both could love.

"Come on, pal," he said, grabbing the leash. "Let's take you out for a walk. It's going to be a long day in that car."

Gwen was at the breakfast table finishing her coffee when they returned home. Even after the awful night they'd had, Todd thought, she still looked beautiful, her blond hair tumbling carelessly over the silk robe that hung from her perfect shoulders. At times like this, he almost couldn't believe his good fortune. For a formerly nerdy kid, having a girlfriend like Gwen was a dream come true.

As the garage door closed behind him, she looked up and gave him a wan smile.

"Where were you?"

"Taking Archie for a walk."

Todd was tempted to tell her about the scene at the dog park, Archie going down the slide, giving high fives, and playing leapfrog with the kids, but he didn't want to make things worse. There was still a part of him that hoped Gwen would change her mind, but that wouldn't happen if she thought she was being pressured.

"Did you call Claire?"

He poured himself some coffee and took a seat.

"I did," he said.

"And . . . ?"

"She says she's willing to take him, if we want her to."

"You're not still thinking of keeping him, are you?"

"No, not really."

Todd took a sip. The coffee that morning seemed especially bitter.

"I told her we'd drive him out today," he said. "If we leave soon, I think we can get there before dark."

Gwen hooked a golden curl behind her ear.

"I'm not spending the entire day in that smelly car."

He took another sip of coffee and shook his head.

"I thought we'd take your car."

"You want to put *that dog* in my brand-new Audi?"

"Why not?"

Her lips pursed. "Um, because it's my car?"

Todd stared at her. Why the attitude all of a sudden? Yes, Archie had made a mess in the car, but it was Todd's fault for leaving him alone with the chicken. And he'd already given the dog a bath, so it wasn't as if he'd be stinking up the Audi. As for the Volvo, Todd would make an appointment with the detailer to have it cleaned. Once that was done, it'd be fine.

"Well," he said, "we have to get him out to Claire's somehow."

"No, *you* have to get him there." Gwen stood and poured herself another cup of coffee. "*I'm* spending the weekend with Dad and Tippi."

Todd could feel his temper rise. Whenever the two of them had an argument, Gwen's first impulse was always to go running back to her father and stepmother.

"But we have reservations at Shiro's on Sunday."

"So? We can go next weekend."

He stared at the table, wondering what to do. If he told

Gwen why he was taking her to Shiro's, he'd spoil the surprise, but if he didn't, she'd head off to her parents' house to sulk. The frustration must have shown on his face; Gwen set a hand on his shoulder and squeezed.

"Look, I'm sorry, but this really is your mess to clean up. If you'd called and asked me first, it would have saved us both a lot of grief."

As unhappy as he was with the way things were turning out, Todd had to admit that Gwen was right. It had been thoughtless of him to expect her to welcome a new pet without any warning. Why should she have to help him drive Archie out to Claire's? Still, the last thing he wanted was to put off his proposal. He reached up and took her hand.

"At least let me make it up to you by taking you to Shiro's, okay?"

Gwen withdrew her hand.

"No, Daddy and Tips are having a party; I doubt I'll be leaving before the last ferry sails." She leaned over and kissed the top of his head. "But don't worry, I should be back on Monday."

Monday. Todd sighed. Maybe he should just ask Gwen now and get it over with.

No, he thought, he wanted to do this right. A proposal wasn't something you did on the spur of the moment; it was the first step in a life together. If he couldn't make it work this weekend as planned, then he'd just have to wait. Another week wouldn't kill him, he told himself. Even if, at that moment, it felt like it would.

Todd left Gwen to finish her breakfast and headed upstairs to pack. Ordinarily, he wouldn't have bothered for just one night, but there was always a chance he'd run into some snow on the way out to Claire's. Best to have some extra clothes for the cold weather.

He went to the guest room closet and took down the suit-case he'd gotten for Christmas—one of a matched set from Gwen's father—and set it out on the bed. It wasn't something Todd would have chosen for himself, but the lock was impregnable and you could run the darned thing over with a tank without making a dent in it. As he leaned against its rigid frame, he felt something small and square dig into his thigh.

Todd reached into his pocket and pulled out the velvet box that held Gwen's engagement ring. With all the commotion the night before, he hadn't thought to put it away, and when he got up that morning, he'd simply pulled on the same pair of pants he'd worn to the funeral. It was strange, he thought. As obsessed as he'd been about proposing to Gwen, he'd completely forgotten about the ring.

He was about to put it back in his dresser when something told him to wait. It was possible that Gwen might go looking for something and discover it by accident, of course, but it wasn't the fear of having her spoil his surprise that was stopping him.

Their disagreement over Archie had shaken Todd. If the two of them couldn't agree on something that simple, he wondered, what else would they disagree about in the future? And would those arguments always be settled in the same way, with Todd backing down and Gwen emerging victorious?

"Maybe I'll just take this with me," he told himself, and slipped it into the suitcase's zipper compartment.

Half an hour later, Todd and Archie were on the road. With his Volvo still covered in chicken fat and Gwen's car unavailable, Todd had decided to take his Jeep. The old Cherokee XJ had been his father's pride and joy, and when Todd acquired it at sixteen, he'd vowed never to give it up. Gwen refused to be seen in it, but Todd loved the rugged old four-by-four. When he was behind the wheel, it felt like nothing in the world could hold him back.

Archie sat up in the passenger's seat, his ears cocked forward, watching the world whiz by. Todd had briefly considered putting him in the carrier, but it seemed cruel to confine the dog in such a small space for so long. The lamb's-wool seat covers were practically indestructible and a lot more comfortable to sit on, and besides, Todd enjoyed having some company up front.

"I was thinking we'd take 522 out to Monroe and then 2 east to Claire's place," Todd said. "Does that sound good to you?"

Archie barked his approval, adding a quick tail wag for emphasis.

"All right, then." Todd smiled. "It's all settled."

Getting such a late start, however, meant that it wasn't long before traffic got heavy, and by eleven, northbound traffic was at a standstill. Todd took out his phone and checked the road conditions. Twenty miles of construction, a five-mile detour, and a three-car accident lay between where they were and Claire's house, and that didn't even include the regular maintenance crews whose Day-Glo vests always seemed to make drivers slow down and gawk. Todd sighed.

Of all the weekends to be out on the road.

He called Claire to give her his revised ETA.

"I don't think we're going to make it in time for dinner," he said. "I got a late start and traffic is miserable."

"How's the weather where you are?"

"Fine," he said. "Why?"

"Bob just told me we've got ice pellets coming down out here. You might want to find a place to stay the night and start out again in the morning."

"I think we'll be okay, but if anything changes I'll give you a call."

"How's Gwen holding up?"

"She, um, didn't come."

Imagining the look on his sister's face, he braced for a scathing comeback.

"I'll keep your dinner warm for you," she said. "Just drive carefully, okay?"

"Will do," he said. "Thanks."

Todd looked at the phone.

Well, that was different.

"Looks like it'll be slow going for a while," he told Archie. "Feel free to make yourself comfortable."

The little dog glanced from Todd to the stationary cars around them and back again, as if confirming that there was, indeed, nothing much to look at. Then he yawned expansively, smacked his lips, and curled up on the seat, pausing a moment before he closed his eyes.

"Don't worry," Todd said. "I'll let you know if anything exciting happens."

While Archie dozed and the Jeep crept forward, Todd thought about what had just happened on the phone. Claire had been going out of her way to be hostile to his girlfriend since the moment they met, but she'd just been given the perfect opportunity to unload on Gwen and hadn't taken it. What had changed?

Maybe, he thought, it had something to do with their conversation the day before. Todd had suspected for years that Claire was nursing a grudge about his so-called abandonment of Emma Carlisle. Being younger, she'd been sheltered from the unpleasant realities of the family's situation after their father's death, and it wouldn't surprise him at all if Claire had misinterpreted his willingness to help out as an excuse to leave Emma behind.

Whatever the reason was, though, he hoped this signaled

the end of Claire's campaign against his girlfriend. Todd was nuts about Gwen. He was determined to marry her, and his sister's complaint that she only cared about money was ridiculous—Gwen's family was loaded! Sure, she talked a lot about the nice things she had, but that was only because she had a lot of nice things to talk about. Deep down, Gwen was no more materialistic than anyone else, and once she realized that Todd's desire for a simpler, slower-paced life was sincere, he knew she'd be as excited about the possibilities as he was.

After forty minutes of crawling along, the snarled traffic suddenly evaporated and the Jeep began to pick up speed. By then, however, the sky had darkened and it wasn't long before rain was pelting down. The sound of the windshield wipers woke Archie from his nap. He stood up on the seat, put his paws on the dashboard, and stared avidly at their back-and-forth motion.

"Careful," Todd told him. "Don't give yourself a stiff neck."

The rain would slow them down a bit, he thought, but at least they were moving forward again. As they passed the first construction zone without incident, Todd began to feel more confident about their prospects for reaching Claire's house that night. Unfortunately, the sound of water sluicing along the car had a predictable effect on both man and dog, and it wasn't long before they were searching for a rest stop.

"And maybe a McDonald's, too," Todd said, peering through the downpour. "I don't know about you, but I'm starved."

CHAPTER 6

"Excuse me, Miss Carlisle, have you got a moment? There's a little problem I need to discuss with you."

Emma had just gotten to work that morning when her handyman, Jake, showed up. Finding Jake at her office door was always unsettling. He cared more about the inn than anyone other than Clifton and herself, but he had yet to come to her with a "little problem" that had cost her less than a thousand dollars. Given the inn's precarious financial situation, she'd been hoping the two of them could remain strangers for at least a few more months. She invited him to take a seat and closed the door.

"What's on your mind?" she said.

"It's the roof. You remember there was a problem after that windstorm in August?"

"Right. We lost some shakes over the east wing. I thought that was fixed."

"It was," he said. "But at the time, I warned you that the underlying structure was unsound. We need to shore up that roof before the rains start up in earnest or the water'll eat right through the ceiling below."

"That's over the Spirit Room, isn't it?"

"Right."

Emma considered that for a moment. It wasn't only rain that was the problem. Once snow started falling, every cubic foot of accumulation would place fifteen to twenty pounds of pressure on the already-weakened roof. If it caved in, water damage would be the least of her worries.

"How bad is it leaking now?"

Jake shrugged. "No way to tell for sure without cutting a hole in the roof and sending the scope down."

"You still haven't found the door to that part of the attic, I take it?"

"No, ma'am. Whoever built this place had some pretty strange ideas about construction."

She nodded. It wasn't the first time they'd had this problem. Old buildings weren't made to conform to modern codes, and when they were built for people with more money than sense, they could be downright bizarre. No wonder everyone thought the Spirit Inn was haunted.

"Have you got any idea what it would take to fix it?" she said.

Jake considered that awhile.

"No," he said. "But it's probably going to be a bigger job than I can do on my own; the damage could go all the way to the ceiling. Even if it doesn't, though, I'll still need somebody to give me a hand."

Emma bit her lip. Hiring someone with the right skills who was willing to take a temporary position wasn't going to be easy—or cheap. She knew Jake resented being the last one on her priority list, but if he'd just stick it out a little longer, she swore she'd make it up to him.

"I'll tell you what," she said. "I've applied for another loan at the bank; I should hear from them in the next few days.

Until then, why don't you throw a tarp over the damaged area and give me an estimate for the work that needs to be done?"

Jake was clearly unhappy about her refusal.

"It won't be worth the paper it's written on if I can't get in there and take a look first," he grumbled.

"Then just do the best you can." She glanced at the door. "Listen, I have to make sure that things are ready for tonight. Let me think about this some more and we'll talk about it again on Monday, okay?"

"Fine," he said. "Monday, then."

Jake walked out of the office and closed the door more firmly than necessary.

Just what she needed, Emma thought, another expense. When was the place going to stop being a money pit? She set her elbows on the desk and massaged her temples. It was times like these when Emma missed her grandmother the most. *"You could sell it, take the money, and see the world."*

Her banker's words came back to her as Emma stared down at her desk. Hardly a week went by when she didn't get a call from a developer asking if she'd be willing to sell. It was getting so that the natural beauty of the area was something only the ultrarich could enjoy. The ski lodges were bad enough, but tens of thousands of acres had been bought up and fenced off by high-tech millionaires who built enormous "cabins" that remained vacant most of the year. The way she saw it, if she sold out there'd be that much less for regular folks.

She sat up straight and took a deep breath. *It doesn't matter,* Emma thought. She'd been through a lot worse: a troubled childhood, her mother's overdose, abusive boyfriends. She was determined to make this place work. Her loan was going to be approved, the roof would get fixed, and the problem that was eating up her profits would be resolved. In the meantime, there were guests who needed her. She would not let them down.

Emma took a peek in the mirror before heading out. As she adjusted her ascot, she wondered if the whole Victorian theme was really worth the bother. The jackets the staff wore had to be custom-tailored, and although the dry-cleaning bills weren't ex-orbitant, it would be a lot cheaper if they switched to outfits that could be laundered in-house. Clifton had nearly had a stroke when she mentioned the possibility, but sooner or later he'd have to admit that if they wanted to put the inn on a stronger financial footing, they'd have to start thinking outside the box. If he was going to insist that Jean-Paul be more frugal with the kitchen staples, he had to be ready to make a few sac-rifices himself.

Adam was alone at the front desk when she walked out. Emma looked around.

"Where's Clifton?" she said.

He shrugged. "He took off when you got here."

She nodded absently. Clifton never seemed to stop pa-trolling the inn. At least once a day, it seemed, he would run off and neither Emma nor anyone else would be able to find him. Then a few hours later he'd turn up, having inspected the grounds, tested the water pressure in one of the rooms, or inventoried the staples in the pantry. Emma had spent years working at the inn, but she'd have bet there were still places Clifton had been that she didn't know existed.

And even he can't find the door to the attic.

"Well, if you see him again, will you tell him to come find me? I'm going down to the conference rooms."

"Sure thing," Adam said. "By the way, thanks for the help last night. Guess I'm still a little slow."

"You were doing fine," she said. "I just needed something to do."

Emma struck out across the lobby, waving at familiar faces and exchanging a word or two with those she'd missed the night before. A woman visiting for the first time said she was interested in nineteenth-century Queen Anne buildings, and while the two of them discussed the finer points of Eastlake versus Gothic Revival influence on American Victorian architecture, Emma took a look at the ceiling. Whatever might be wrong with the roof over the Spirit Room, she thought, at least it wasn't evident in there.

She checked the banquet room, making sure the tables and chairs had been set up, the place settings were all arranged, and the decorations were complete. Then Emma spent several minutes walking around the Spirit Room, inspecting its ceiling from every angle. There was a slight bow in the middle and a few superficial cracks that had probably been there for years, but no signs of mold or water damage. That didn't mean that her handyman was wrong, of course, but it did ease her mind a bit. For the time being, at least, they wouldn't have to set out buckets to catch any leaks. And who knew? Maybe Jake would drop his camera inside and find that there wasn't much to repair after all.

When she'd finished her inspection, Emma went back to the banquet room and asked one of the waitresses if she'd seen Clifton. The woman told her that he'd dropped by the kitchen for a short time about ten minutes before but that no one had seen him since. As Emma stood there amid the occult-themed décor, she wondered if her assistant manager might actually be one of the ghosts that were said to inhabit the Spirit Inn. It certainly would explain a lot.

CHAPTER 7

Todd and Archie were finally off the Interstate and the Jeep was making good time when his phone rang. It was Claire.

"Where are you?"

"Almost to Monroe," he said. "We got hung up in traffic and took the detour from hell. Why?"

"The weather out here is getting worse. The highway patrol is advising all nonemergency vehicles to stay off the roads until tomorrow afternoon."

Todd looked out his windshield at a garden-variety rainstorm.

"It doesn't look that bad here."

"Yeah, but you're about five thousand feet below us. Once you get past Gold Bar, things are going to get ugly."

"Crap."

They'd gone too far to turn around, Todd thought. He and Archie would just have to stop for the night.

"So, what do you want to do?" she said.

"We'll have to find a place to stay, I guess. Know any motels out here that allow pets?"

"There's the Dog Days Inn. It's about five miles past Monroe."

Todd chuckled. "The Dog Days Inn, huh? What's it like?"

"We've never stayed there, but Bob knows a guy at work who has. He says it's all right."

"I'll check it out. Thanks."

"I'm sorry," she said. "I hate to leave you in the lurch."

"No problem," he told her. "Not much either of us can do about the weather. I'll talk to you later."

When they hung up, Todd looked up directions to the Dog Days Inn. Google Maps said it was about seven minutes away. Yelp gave it two stars.

Oh well, he thought. *You can't expect five-star accommodations at a pet-friendly hotel.* Besides, it was only for one night. How bad could it be?

But when he pulled into the hotel's gravel driveway, Todd's optimism faltered. What had appeared on the Internet to be a quaint Swiss chalet was actually a one-story cinder-block building with a white clapboard façade, green shutters, and a peaked roof made of corrugated steel. The Jeep rolled to a stop.

"Well, what do you think?"

Archie put his nose to the window and the two of them stared out at the peeling paint, damaged siding, and weeds growing along the foundation.

"Yeah," Todd said. "It's a little run-down."

He pointed.

"And there's some dog doo over there . . . plus a few beer cans and cigarette butts."

Archie shrank back.

"Tell you what," Todd said. "You wait here while I go in and take a look. Maybe it's not so bad inside."

He stepped out and made his way carefully toward the front door.

The first thing Todd noticed was the smell: a disagreeable blend of urine, smoke, and pine cleaner. The olive-green carpet was a patchwork of stains and cigarette burns and the furnishings looked like garage sale castoffs. Even so, the place was pretty busy. There was a play area just off the lobby with balls, chew toys, and a couch. A bored-looking teenager sat by the entrance, watching two bull terriers eviscerate one of the couch's seat cushions.

Todd walked up to the counter and asked if there was a nonsmoking room available.

The desk clerk was reading the *Daily Racing Form*. He turned the page.

"We don't have any nonsmoking rooms."

That was surprising. Todd was pretty sure the law required every hotel in the state to have smoke-free accommodations.

The man looked up. "There's a bed and a toilet in every room, but technically this is a kennel, not a hotel."

A kennel? This guy had to be kidding. Still, Todd thought, he and Archie would need someplace to stay the night, and the weather was only going to get worse. He figured one night wouldn't kill either of them.

"All right, I'll take one of those."

"Sorry," the man said, returning his attention to the racing form. "We're all full."

"But the sign out front says 'Vacancy.'" Todd pointed.

The clerk reached over and flipped a switch on the wall.

"No, it doesn't."

They drove for another half an hour trying to find a place that was pet friendly. As the elevation climbed and the sky grew darker, Todd began to lose hope. Archie, too, seemed upset; the little dog shifted in his seat, whining and refusing to settle. It had been a long time since their last break. Todd figured it was time to look for a rest stop.

"How about a walk?" he said. "The rain's letting up. I bet we'll both feel better after we've stretched our legs."

As it happened, there was a rest stop at the next exit, but as Todd pulled off the highway, Archie's agitation increased. He put his paws on the dashboard and began to bark.

"Hold on," Todd said. "Let me at least stop first."

But instead of calming down, Archie started digging at the door panel. As the Jeep turned into the parking lot, Todd felt a rush of cold air and saw the passenger window start to open.

"Whoa, hold on! Archie, stop!"

He lunged across the center console, grabbing for the little dog's collar, but it was too late. With a yelp, Archie launched himself out of the open window and dashed off. Todd slammed on the brakes, but by the time he got out of the Jeep, the little dog was gone.

"Archie! Archie, where are you?"

It had been an hour since his uncle's dog had disappeared. An hour Todd had spent tramping through the woods, following what he thought might be Archie's tracks, and slowly losing hope that he would find the little dog before sundown. He pushed a branch aside and stumbled over an exposed tree root, barely regaining his balance in time to keep from toppling over. The farther he went, the darker it became and the harder it was to tell if the marks on the ground had been made by a small dog or a wild animal. Todd stopped and looked around at the increasingly dense underbrush, wondering if he should keep going or return to the Jeep. If he could just sit down and rest a minute, he thought, maybe he could figure out what to do next.

There's a fallen log up there on the right, just past the next turn.

Goaded by his inexplicable certainty, Todd pushed on and found the log about forty yards ahead. He stood there staring down at it, wondering why he'd been so sure the log was in that exact place. In a forest that age, of course, there was a good chance he'd find fallen logs every so often, but this wasn't the first time in the last few minutes that he'd known what lay just around the next corner. It was as if he was experiencing déjà vu over and over again. He couldn't shake the feeling that he'd been there before.

The undergrowth was thinner there, and Todd saw a light coming from somewhere up ahead. He hesitated, thinking it might be better just to go back to the parking lot than to take a chance, but decided to push on. If he'd noticed the light, maybe Archie had, too. With luck, they'd find shelter—and each other—there.

His first glimpse of the Spirit Inn nearly took Todd's breath away; the place was lit up like a Christmas tree. It had been years since he'd been there, but the inn hadn't changed a bit. The garden wasn't as green as it had been in the summer, of course, and the pool was covered for the season, but the old building looked pretty much the same. If he walked through the front door blindfolded, he thought, he'd probably still be able to find his way around.

The paw prints he'd been following were nowhere in sight, but that didn't mean Archie couldn't have been there, and Todd was curious to take a look inside. He headed around to the front door to see if anyone had reported seeing a small dog in the area.

After he'd seen how little the outside of the inn had changed, stepping into the lobby was a shock. The comfortable, homey décor Todd remembered had been replaced by antique furniture, intricate stained glass, and heavy velvet curtains. One thing that hadn't changed, though, was the clerk at the front desk.

The man was older now and the green jacket was new, but Todd would never forget that hair and mustache.

As he approached the desk, the man gave him a cool, unfriendly smile and Todd realized how scruffy he must look after tramping through the woods. He ran a hand through his hair and shrugged apologetically.

"May I help you?" the man said.

"I'm looking for my dog."

"I'm afraid we don't allow dogs here."

The man's attitude was as intimidating as ever. It made Todd feel like he was twelve again, asking if his room key was in the Lost and Found. Why had he even gone inside? It wasn't as if Archie could have walked in on his own.

"Sorry." Todd shook his head. "I'm Todd Dwyer. I don't know if you remember me, but my family used to vacation here a lot when I was a kid."

The man's expression remained unchanged.

"Uh, right," Todd said.

This is awkward.

"You see, I was at the rest stop down the hill and my dog ran off. I thought one of your guests might have—"

"Clifton, when you've got a minute, can I—?"

A small, slim woman in a green blazer had poked her head out of the door behind the front desk. Todd felt his heart leap.

Emma?

"Oh," she said, ducking back. "Sorry."

"I'll be right with you," the clerk said. "Mr. Dwyer here was just leaving."

The woman paused and took a second look at Todd. He grinned, and a sly smile spread across her face.

"Wasn't there a Dwyer family who used to come here in the summer? They had a sweet girl named Claire and a rude little boy named Todd."

Clifton spluttered, horrified; then Todd and Emma began to laugh.

"Oh, I see," he said. "It's a joke."

Emma came around the desk and shook Todd's hand.

"It's good to see you again, Todd. How are you?"

"Fine," he said, feeling oddly let down by the handshake. "So you're working here now, huh?"

"Actually," she said, "I own it."

"*Own* it? What happened to your Gran?"

Emma sobered. "She passed away last year."

"Oh. I'm sorry."

"No, it's all right," she said. "What about you? How's your family?"

Todd shrugged. "Dad's gone. He had a heart attack about a month after our last visit."

"I'm sorry to hear that," Emma said. "He was always very kind to me."

"Yeah," Todd said. "He was a great guy." He swallowed. "Anyway, Claire's all grown up and has twin boys now."

"No way! And your mom?"

"Same as ever; loves being a grandma; lots of hints being dropped about me getting married."

Todd felt his face redden. Why had he said that?

If Emma noticed, however, she didn't show it.

"I guess that's the upside of being an orphan," she said. "Nobody trying to push me down the aisle." She looked around. "Are you checking in?"

"Actually, I came by to see if anyone had seen my dog. He got away from me at the rest stop down the hill. I was following his tracks when I realized I was close to the inn, so I thought I'd stop by and see if he'd come this way."

Emma turned to Clifton.

"Have you checked with the staff to see if anyone's seen Mr. Dwyer's dog . . . ?"

She looked back at Todd.

"Archie," he said.

Clifton picked up the phone. "I'll call housekeeping."

Emma smiled. "Why don't I drive you back to the rest stop so you can get your car? Maybe he'll have turned up by the time we get back."

She went back to her office and grabbed her keys.

"Do you live around here?" she asked as they headed out to the parking lot.

"No," Todd said. "I was on my way out to Claire's. They live up near Monte Cristo."

Emma gave him a worried look.

"You weren't planning to get there tonight, were you? I hear the roads are pretty slick up north."

He shook his head. "No, we were going to spend the night someplace around here and try again tomorrow. Now, though, I'm not sure what I'm going to do."

"Why don't you stay with us?" she said. "My treat."

Todd glanced back at the inn.

"I thought you didn't allow pets."

"Not in the hotel, but if you find him, Archie can stay with me. I live in the old cottage out back."

"I remember that cottage!" Todd said. "It was always crammed full of old junk."

Emma laughed. "Yeah, well, I cleaned it out. Now it's crammed full of new junk."

CHAPTER 8

Emma kept stealing glances at Todd while she drove to the rest stop. It was hard to believe she'd just been thinking about him and now there he was in the flesh. Of course, it wasn't as if he'd come there to see her, but after the way things between them had ended, she never imagined she'd see him again.

It had been thirteen years, she thought. Thirteen long years since they'd seen each other. A lot had happened since then.

Emma had still been living with her mother back then, moving from place to place, changing schools twice or three times a year, and spending her summers working at the inn and trying to piece together enough of what she'd gleaned in the classroom to keep from being held back the next school year. She'd eventually graduated, gone to college, and been in and out of some bad relationships, but on the outside, she really hadn't changed all that much. Todd, on the other hand, looked like a completely different person.

He'd been a skinny teenager with thick glasses back then, a shy boy who'd struggled to keep up with her as they roamed the backwoods, climbing trees and jumping streams. Now Todd was a head taller, the glasses were gone, and she could tell there was muscle under the old sweatshirt he was wearing. As Emma watched him from the corner of her eye, she wondered if his memories of her were as fond as the ones she had of him.

"I still can't believe you own the old inn," he said.

"Yeah, there'd been some hints over the years, but I never thought Gran was serious about leaving it to me. It felt like winning the lottery."

"When I saw it from the trail, it was as if I'd just left. The outside looks exactly the way I remembered it."

"There have been a few changes," she said, "but you're right. The building is pretty much the same as when your family was here last."

He cleared his throat, looking shamefaced.

"I'm sorry you never heard from me. Things got pretty hairy after my dad died. He didn't believe in life insurance and we didn't have much in savings. I pretty much became the man of the house."

"Forget about it." She glanced at him. "It was a long time ago."

"It wasn't really my choice," he added hastily. "I wanted to write, but my mother wouldn't let me."

Emma smirked. If there was one thing she'd learned from her Gran, it was that you don't blame others for your bad behavior.

"What did she do? Lock up all the pens and paper?"

She'd said it without thinking and it surprised her to hear how much venom there was in her voice.

"No, but she asked me not to," he said. "What else could I do?"

"Oh, I don't know. What does the man of the house usually do?"

Todd's face clouded. "I said I was sorry."

"I know." Emma softened. "I guess I was just a little more upset about it than I thought. Apology accepted."

There followed a few minutes of uncomfortable silence. Emma felt sorry for giving Todd a hard time, but it wasn't as if her life had been any easier back then. Had it never occurred to him that sharing their experiences might have helped them both? Still, she thought, it wasn't her place to criticize, especially now, when he'd just lost his dog.

She began scanning the woods on either side of them.

"What does this dog of yours look like, anyway?"

"He's small, with kind of wiry white fur, and he's got a tan patch over one eye, but if he's been running around in the mud, you might not be able to tell."

"Any particular breed?"

"Nope. Just a mutt."

The turnoff for the rest stop was ahead on the right. As Emma drove into the parking lot, her truck's headlights swept across the only other vehicle there—an old Jeep Cherokee covered in road grime. It had to be at least fifteen years old, she thought, feeling a bit let down. Todd must not be doing so well.

"Is that yours?" she said.

"Yeah."

Emma pulled into the space next to the Jeep and looked around. The rest stop had a wide grassy area that sloped sharply downward about fifty feet from the parking lot. There were bathrooms off to the left and a couple of picnic tables on either side of the concrete path that divided the space down the middle. If there was a dog out there, however, she didn't see any evidence of him.

"Where were you guys when he got away?"

"Right here," Todd said. "I hadn't even stopped before Archie opened the window and took off."

Emma looked at him. "He opened the window by himself?"

"Yeah. I thought maybe it was an accident at first, but now I wonder if it was something he learned from Uncle Bertie."

"Wait a minute. Is this the Uncle Bertie who was a circus clown?"

Todd laughed. "Did I tell you about him?"

"Oh, my gosh. I used to think that was the coolest thing I'd ever heard of. For years, I wanted to join the circus like your uncle did. Is he still performing?"

"No," Todd said. "He died last week. That's how I got Archie."

"Oh, Todd." Emma put her hand on his shoulder. "I'm sorry."

She paused for a moment.

"Wait a minute. You mean Archie's still alive? He must be ancient."

"No, this is a different Archie. Uncle Bertie had a whole series of dogs with that name."

"And they were all circus dogs?"

"Pretty much. This last one mostly did kids' birthday parties, but he knows a lot of tricks."

"Well, even a smart dog can get lost in the woods," she said, reaching over and grabbing the flashlight from her glove box. "Come on. Let's go take a look."

They searched the rest stop for twenty minutes while the dusk deepened and the rain intensified. Todd and Emma yelled themselves hoarse calling for the little dog, but Archie either couldn't hear them or didn't want to be found. When the two of them finally turned and trudged back to the truck, the only sound they heard was the squelching of their shoes.

Todd looked dispirited. "Do you mind if we wait a few more minutes? He might still turn up."

"Okay," she said. "But let's get back in the truck. My teeth are starting to chatter."

Emma started the engine and turned on the heat. It didn't take long before the windows began to fog up.

"I'll fix that," he said.

Todd stripped off his wet sweatshirt, revealing a T-shirt underneath that clung to him like a second skin. As he started wiping down the glass, Emma tried not to stare.

"I can have housekeeping launder that when we get back, if you'd like."

He shrugged. "That's okay. I've got plenty of dry clothes in the Jeep."

As Todd worked his way across the windshield, she kept her eyes on the trail that had led him to the inn. There was no sign of anything even remotely resembling a small white dog out there, but at least it distracted her from ogling Todd.

I've been alone too long, Emma thought. *I'm becoming shameless.*

"You see something?" he said, following her gaze.

Emma shook her head. "Nope. I don't see anything."

Todd sat back and tossed his sweatshirt onto the floor. Between the effort of looking for Archie and clearing the windows, he'd begun to sweat, and in the close confines of the truck's cab, Emma found the effect intoxicating. There was something she still found very attractive about Todd, she realized, and bit her lip. He wasn't wearing a wedding ring, either, which was encouraging. What was it he'd said about his mother bugging him to get married?

Whoa, slow down, girl! Let's not get ahead of ourselves.

"Why don't we head back?" she said. "Maybe someone's seen him up at the inn."

"Maybe." Todd was still watching the woods. "The inside seemed a lot different, but maybe I'm just misremembering."

It took her a second to figure out that he was talking about the inn. *He doesn't want to give up yet,* she thought. *He's stalling for time.*

"You're right," she said. "When business started going down-hill about eight years ago, Gran decided to come up with a theme that would attract new customers. She and Clifton liked the idea of tying it in with the age of the building—"

"Hence the Victorian stuff."

"Right. The antiques, the stained glass, all the period pieces you see in the lobby, are in the rooms, too. And everything just clicked when she discovered that the place was haunted."

Todd's head swiveled. "Haunted? You're kidding."

"Nope. Gran and Clifton did some digging into the history of the inn and found out about it. We've had people come from all over the world hoping to encounter one of our ghosts."

"And do they?"

"Who knows?" She shrugged. "I've never encountered one myself."

"So the new theme worked."

Emma paused, thinking about her current financial struggles.

"More or less. I worry sometimes that we're dependent upon a pretty limited clientele, but they're loyal and it's hard try-ing to differentiate yourself from the big chains."

He looked back out the window.

"I can imagine."

"So," Emma said, "what are you doing with yourself these days?"

Todd hesitated, looking uncomfortable.

"I'm in a period of transition at the moment," he said. "I left my old job a few months ago and now I work at home part-time."

Emma nodded. *Well, that settles it,* she thought. A period of transition? Working part-time from home? Todd was definitely down on his luck. She sighed. *Why am I always attracted to the losers?*

Todd set his hand on the door.

"I'd better let you get back to work. I'll get the Jeep warmed up and follow you in a few minutes."

As the door clicked open, he shook his head.

"I keep thinking that Archie must have seen a squirrel," he said. "Why else would a dog just take off like that?"

Emma shrugged. "Maybe he saw a ghost."

CHAPTER 9

By the time Todd stepped into his hotel room, he was exhausted. It had been a long day of driving on top of a pretty sleepless night when Archie ran away, and that had been more than two hours ago. Cold, hungry, and sick with worry, he was too tired to set his burden down gently. He opened his hands and let the suitcase and dog carrier crash to the floor.

Archie might be trapped somewhere, he thought, or hurt. A coyote or a black bear could have eaten him. Had he run out onto the highway and been hit by a car? Was he shivering and wet, in danger of starving to death? The myriad ways a little dog could be killed or injured flashed through Todd's mind like a montage of disaster.

Cut it out. All you're doing is borrowing trouble.

He stripped off his clothing and stepped into the shower. Once he was clean and wearing warmer clothes, he'd get himself some dinner and figure out what to do next. There had to be an emergency vet or an animal shelter around somewhere. He'd give them a call and see if anyone had brought in a small white dog. After that, well, who knew?

At least he had a place to stay that wasn't a smelly, rundown kennel. When Todd thought about the Dog Days Inn, it made him shudder. He'd probably be spending the night in his Jeep if Emma hadn't offered to take Archie in. Todd hoped she knew how grateful he was. He could never have left the area without knowing what had happened to the little dog.

He dried himself off and put on the complimentary robe that was hanging on the back of the door, then walked out to the bedroom, picked up his suitcase, and keyed in the four-digit security code. It was ridiculous having luggage that was as impregnable as Fort Knox. Todd would have exchanged it for something simpler, but Gwen's father had made a big deal about that particular feature and he knew the old man would take it personally if he found out Todd had gotten rid of it—which he would. Living with Gwen was like having her father's spy in the house.

The suitcase didn't open.

Maybe his fingers were damp. Todd wiped his hand on the robe and tried a second time. Once again, the lock refused to budge. He tried a third time and swore in frustration when it didn't open. Even the correct combination wouldn't work now, he thought. After three incorrect entries, the lock required a one-hour time-out. Todd was too tired and too hungry to deal with another setback just then. There was a restaurant just off the lobby. He glanced at the pile of damp clothing on the floor.

Or maybe I'll just call room service.

While he waited for his food to arrive, Todd took a tour of the room. He was tempted to stretch out on the bed, but he knew that the second his head hit the pillow he'd be wrecked and there was still too much to do before he could let himself sleep. Besides, he was curious to see what a so-called haunted hotel room looked like.

Emma's grandmother had furnished the place with some very nice Victoriana. Mostly reproduction pieces, but a couple of curios on the nightstand looked as if they might be the real

thing. As he crossed the room to the window, he suddenly realized that he'd been in this room before. It surprised him, too,
because he and his family had never rented a single when they
stayed at the inn. His mother had always insisted they get a
suite so that the four of them could stay in the same room.

So why was this one so familiar? The same feeling he'd had
out in the woods came back to him. He was sure he'd been in
there before. Todd scanned the room, searching his memory for
a clue. Was it in the closet? He opened the door and winced.
Even after all these years, the smell of cedar was as bracing as
smelling salts.

He found what he was looking for at the back of the closet.
Crudely carved into the cedar lining, two sets of initials—his
and Emma's—that he'd put there the summer he turned four-
teen, their secret hidden from prying eyes. For years, Todd had
put any thoughts of the Spirit Inn out of his mind. Now he
found himself flooded with happy memories.

He'd been eleven the first time he met Emma. She was a
year younger than he was, and he remembered his mother
commenting that she looked small and underfed. If she was,
though, he'd never have known it. Back then, Emma wore a
knife strapped to her right leg, "just in case," and could climb
a tree like a monkey. Todd had thought her very brave. In sub-
sequent years, she dropped the tough-kid act, but she was
never completely at ease around other people. The summer he
turned thirteen, Todd spent the entire week trying to work up
the courage to kiss Emma, only to have her punch him in the
stomach when he finally did. The year he turned sixteen was
the last time they were together, and by then their friendship
had blossomed into something that felt a lot like love. Since
then, those summers at the Spirit Inn seemed more like fairy
tales than something that had actually happened.

Todd ran his index finger over the letters he'd carved in the fragrant wood. Seeing Emma again had been a pleasant surprise. From the little his mother had told him about her circumstances, he knew she'd had a tough childhood and he was glad she'd gotten a chance to make something of herself. A few breaks in life could make the difference between doing well and falling to the bottom. It was nice to know that Emma was the kind of person who'd make the most of any breaks she got.

There was a knock on the door. He ducked out of the closet and let the waiter in. As the man set the table and laid out the covered dishes, Todd felt his mouth begin to water. He reached for his wallet and the waiter shook his head.

"Compliments of the house."

Todd stood there awkwardly, so focused on the food that he was temporarily at a loss. Then he took out a ten, handed it to the man, and hustled him out the door.

"Thank you, sir," the waiter said. "Enjoy your meal."

Todd did enjoy his meal, and when it was over he finally allowed himself to lie down. The staff had been told to keep an eye out for Archie and the animal shelters were closed for the night. There wasn't much more he could do for the little dog now but rest and start looking for him again in the morning. He glanced at the suitcase.

Speaking of trying again.

Todd took out his phone and started looking through the list of passwords, log-in IDs, and PIN numbers that he kept there. He found the code for the suitcase and frowned—he'd been entering the right one all along, so why hadn't it worked? He tried it again.

Still no luck. If it had been any other type of case, he could have picked the lock or even broken it to get his things out, but a pipe bomb wouldn't have helped with that thing. Once again, Gwen and her family had put him in a fix.

He looked at the clothes sitting in a heap on the floor. For the time being, at least, they were all he had to wear. Emma had offered to have the housekeeping staff launder them. Maybe it was time to take her up on the offer.

When the housekeeper had gone, Todd got into bed, leaving the robe within easy reach in case someone came to the door. Then he took out his phone and called Gwen. The number rang five times before kicking him over to her voice mail. He left a brief message telling her where he was and that he'd call again in the morning, but didn't say anything about Archie. After the argument they'd had over whether or not to keep him, Todd wasn't sure he wanted to hear Gwen's reaction when she found out the little dog was missing. He supposed his next call should be to Claire, but Todd was reluctant to tell his sister what had happened. She might have held her tongue once, but if she found out that Archie was lost, the gloves would come off. And there was no way he was going to tell her where he was staying, either. Knowing his sister, she'd see it as an open invitation to try to get Todd and Emma back together again. It would be safer, he thought, and much easier just to call his mother and have her pass the news along.

"Where are you staying?" his mother asked when he got her on the phone.

"Do you remember the Spirit Inn?"

"Of course. We stayed there lots of times when your father was alive."

"The rest stop where Archie took off is just down the road from there. I didn't even realize how close it was until I literally walked up to the back door."

"My goodness," she said. "Has it changed much since we were there?"

"Inside it has, yeah. But from the outside it looks exactly the same. Do you remember the owner's granddaughter, Emma?"

There was a pause.

"Yes," she said. "She used to play with you and Claire."

"Well, she owns the place now. We ran into each other in the lobby and she drove me back to the rest stop to help me look for Archie."

"Oh. Well, that was nice of her."

Todd frowned. Had the news about Emma made her uncomfortable, or was he just imagining things?

"Is something wrong?"

"Of course not. Why would there be?"

"No reason."

You're just tired, he told himself. *It's been a long day.*

"Anyway," he said, "she asked about you and Claire and I told her about Dad. She even comped me a room in case Archie shows up."

"Oh, Todd. You didn't let her."

"Don't worry, I'll pay for it. I just didn't want to be rude."

"Well, thank you for checking in. I'll tell Claire you'll call her tomorrow."

"Thanks, Ma."

"It's no problem," she said. "Say hello to Emma for me. Tell her I . . . well, I hope there aren't any hard feelings."

Todd hung up and turned off the light. It was so peaceful at the inn, no traffic on the road outside, none of the chatter and background noise that he took for granted in the city. As he lay there in the dark, lulled by the patter of the rain outside, he felt his body begin to relax.

I could get used to this.

If he and Gwen bought a place out here, he thought, they could enjoy it all the time. With the money he'd made from the sale of his company, Todd would never have to work again, and if he wanted to continue writing game apps, he could do that anywhere. Gwen had been hinting that she might like to quit her job when they had kids, too, and what better place to raise them? The best times he and Claire had ever had were spent in the woods around the Spirit Inn. He couldn't think of a more precious gift to give his own kids than the chance to do the same.

Remembering the good times they'd had, Todd thought of how lucky Emma was to be living there at the inn. It was a job, yes, but one where you could walk out the door at the end of the day and find yourself in the place you loved best in the world. No commute, no waiting for time off so you could cram some relaxation into a week or two before heading back to the grind; just step outside and you're there. No wonder she'd been so forgiving. Who could hold a grudge when they were surrounded by such peace?

He supposed that's why his mother's comment about hard feelings had struck him as so odd. Was she worried that Emma would be angry with him? Well, she had been, briefly, but it hadn't lasted long, and Emma had said nothing to make him think she was mad at his mother. Then Todd thought about how quickly he'd acquiesced when his mother asked him not to write to her all those years before, and it shamed him to realize how cowardly he'd been back then.

No, Ma. Emma's not the one with the hard feelings. I am.

CHAPTER 10

Emma couldn't keep from smiling as she made her final pass through the inn that evening. Seeing Todd again had been like finding a piece of herself that she thought had been lost forever. She told herself that their reunion was only for one day; that Todd wasn't staying for good; that once he found his dog, he'd be off again. But in spite of that, she'd begun fantasizing about what it would be like if he lived there permanently.

He was obviously struggling financially. That old Jeep had to be at least fifteen years old, and the outfit he'd been wearing was barely adequate for the weather. In spite of what he'd told her about having plenty of clothes with him, Emma had found out that he'd asked housekeeping to launder his things so he'd have them to wear in the morning. She wasn't surprised. Emma could still remember a time when she, too, had been too proud to ask for help. In spite of their generous offers, it was often easier to turn to strangers than to friends.

As she stepped into the lobby, she saw the last of the ghost hunters returning to their rooms. The evening's lectures had been over for some time, but it always took at least an hour for everyone to feel as if they'd gotten their money's worth. Her night clerk, Jeremy, was at the front desk, listening as Clifton read out the list of things that needed to be taken care of before morning. As she walked past, she saw the young man stifle a yawn.

Poor guy, she thought. *Good thing it isn't really possible to be bored to death.*

The Van Vandevanders were coming down the hall looking a bit dispirited as they carried the exhibits from Lars's lecture back to their suite. Emma stopped to ask if there was anything she could do.

"No," Lars said. "It's all right. Viv's just feeling a bit deflated at the moment."

Emma glanced at the crestfallen Viv.

"What happened?"

"Nothing," Viv said. "That's the problem. Nothing at all happened. Not last night and not tonight, either."

She sighed dramatically.

"I fear the spirits may have abandoned me."

Lars and Emma exchanged a look. Viv was having her annual moment of doubt. Until one or more ghosts made themselves known to her at the conference, she'd be inconsolable. It had gotten so bad one year that Emma was tempted to rattle a few chains around in the dark just to get Viv out of her funk.

Lars patted his wife's hand.

"My dear, I'm certain that's not the case," he said. "You've had these little dry spells before and they never last."

"But what if this time is different?" she wailed.

"Tut-tut. Be not downhearted. By this time tomorrow, I have no doubt that you'll be 'back in the groove,' as they say."

Viv turned to Emma as if seeking confirmation.

"He's right," Emma said. "It always seems to happen this time of year."

"Really?" Viv turned to her husband. "Is it possible the en-counters are isochronal?"

He frowned thoughtfully. "I don't recall any research on the subject, but I suppose it is possible."

Emma was nonplussed. She hadn't meant for her comment to be taken seriously. Nevertheless, she was glad to have light-ened Viv's gloom, at least temporarily.

"Well," she said, "whatever the reason, I'm sure someone or, er, something will show itself soon."

She gave Viv a hug and continued down the hall, making a brief circuit of the conference rooms before returning to the front desk.

Clifton glanced at her over the top of his reading glasses as she approached.

"I had room service waive the charge for Mr. Dwyer's dinner."

He wrote something on a piece of paper and handed it to Jeremy.

"Poor man looked as if he hadn't eaten all day."

Emma stared. Since when did Clifton show any sympathy for the less fortunate? When Todd showed up that afternoon, it looked as if he'd been ready to toss him out.

"I'm sure he appreciated it," she said.

"It was good of you to offer him a room. Heaven knows where he'd be sleeping tonight otherwise."

She pursed her lips, wondering what was really behind Clifton's comments. Emma would have bet that her assistant manager was promoting some personal agenda. Whatever it was, though, she'd prefer he didn't talk about it in front of their night clerk.

Good grief. He isn't jealous, is he?

"You don't have any objection to Mr. Dwyer's staying here, do you?"

"Hmm?" He looked up. "No, no objection. I was under the impression that you were concerned about the inn's finances, but of course you have every right to treat your beau, if you wish."

She saw Jeremy's eyes widen.

"Todd is an old friend, Cliff. He lost his dog and I thought it would be nice to offer him a place to stay until he finds it."

He looked at her blandly.

"I see."

"And for your information, he's not my *beau*."

"Thank you for telling me. I'm sorry if I upset you."

"You're welcome," she said, trying to regain her composure.

Clifton removed his glasses and tucked them into his breast pocket.

"However, I can't say I'm not relieved," he said. "I'd hate to see you taken advantage of . . . again."

Emma felt her face flush. So there it was, the whole reason for this conversation. Clifton was giving her a not-so-subtle message: *You've screwed up before. Don't let it happen again.*

It was humiliating having her past mistakes thrown in her face, especially in such a sneaky, passive-aggressive way. If Emma tried to call him on it, she was sure that Clifton would deny he'd meant anything of the sort. Emma glanced at Jeremy, whose eyes were practically glued to the paper in front of him, and mustered as much dignity as she could.

"Thank you for your concern," she said. "I think I'll go to my quarters now."

Gran had always told her that the best way to get over an upset was to find a job that needed doing, so the minute Emma got back to the cottage, she changed out of her work clothes and started to clean. First the bathroom, then the kitchen counters;

after that, she swept and vacuumed the floors. She'd been tired before, but after what Clifton had said, she knew she wouldn't sleep until she was ready to drop from exhaustion. As angry as she was, Emma knew that Clifton's words wouldn't have hurt nearly so much if there hadn't been some truth to them. She hadn't always shown good judgment when it came to men, and she'd fallen for some real creeps in the past, but that was behind her and she was smarter now. Besides, Todd wasn't just some guy who'd wandered in off the streets. He and Emma had a history together; they knew each other; they'd been good friends, once.

Once.

Like a fairy tale, she thought. Once upon a time. The fact was, she didn't know anything about the Todd Dwyer who was sleeping up there at her inn. She had no idea what he'd been up to the last thirteen years. He could be a deadbeat dad or a felon or a serial killer for all she knew.

Emma started to laugh. It began as a giggle and grew until she was too weak to stand. She collapsed on the couch and gasped for breath, laughing so hard that tears ran down her cheeks.

A serial killer? Really? Okay, you. Time to go to bed.

She put on her pajamas and pulled out the sofa bed, then snuggled under the covers, enjoying the feeling of content-ment brought on by the belly laugh. She mustn't let Clifton upset her, Emma told herself. She had nothing to apologize for. All she'd done was help out an old friend. If nothing more came of it, that was fine. Emma might be struggling some, but she was a heck of a lot better off than most people. She closed her eyes and thought of all the things she'd do when the bank came through with her loan.

* * *

There was someone at the door. Emma opened her eyes and squinted at the clock: one forty. Who would be banging on her door at this hour? It could be Jeremy, she supposed, if there was an emergency and the phone lines were down, but she still had electricity. She waited a few seconds, expecting to hear a voice. Maybe she'd only dreamed she heard a noise.

No, Emma was sure it was real. It wasn't the rain, or the rustle of tree branches, or even one of the nocturnal animals that occasionally sniffed and scratched at her door. Something out there had made a noise she hadn't heard before outside her cottage. She sat up and strained her hearing, waiting for the slightest hint that whatever it was had not been a delusion.

There it was again, fainter now, but still noticeable—a low moaning sound that made the hair rise on the back of her neck. Emma took a deep breath, reminding herself that, in spite of the Spirit Inn's reputation, there really were no such things as ghosts.

She heard scuffling, then a *thump!* against the door. Emma jumped out of bed and grabbed her robe.

"Who's there?"

She approached the door cautiously and put her eye to the peephole. Nothing. Maybe it was the wind after all.

Thump!

Emma screamed and fell back, her heart pounding. Whatever was out there had jiggled the handle! She searched the room for something to use as a weapon.

"You'd better get out of here," she yelled, grabbing a Merriam-Webster dictionary and raising it to shoulder height. "I've got a gun!"

Well, the word "gun," anyway.

There was more scuffling outside and then Emma heard the unmistakable whimper of a small dog. She gasped.

"Archie?"

She dropped the dictionary and opened her door. A dirty black nose and a face full of matted fur peered up at her.

"Oh, my gosh, it *is* you!"

Emma swung the door wide and Archie limped in. He was wet and shivering and his coat was full of burrs. She closed the door and grabbed a dish towel.

"You poor guy," she said, patting him down gently. "Let's warm you up and get you some food. First things first, though. Let me take a look at that paw."

Emma turned on a light and put Archie in her lap so she could get a better look. His leg felt solid enough, but the fur was matted and mud-covered. Something had forced its way between his toes, but it was hard for her to tell what it was. Judging by the way he'd hobbled through the door, though, she was sure he couldn't get it out by himself.

She hesitated. Emma and Archie were strangers to each other. What if she tried to pull it out and hurt him? She wanted to help, but she didn't feel like being bitten.

"I don't know, fella," she said. "Can I trust you?"

Archie turned and looked at her a long moment, his bright eyes taking her measure. Then he leaned forward and gave her free hand a lick. *Go on,* he seemed to be saying. *I can stand it if you can.*

Emma nodded.

"All right, then," she said. "I'll try to make it quick."

Holding his leg firmly in her left hand, Emma slipped the fingers of the right one under Archie's paw and gently probed the spaces between his leathery pads. She found the problem almost immediately: a spiny cocklebur seed, its razor-sharp spurs buried deep in the tender flesh. Emma marveled that the little dog had been able to walk with that thing in his paw, much less throw himself at her door. You had to admire an animal like that.

She took a deep breath.

"Okay," she told him. "This is going to hurt more for a second, but after that I promise you'll feel a whole lot better. You ready?"

He gave her hand another lick. *I'm ready,* it said. *Let's get this over with.*

When the burr was out, Emma wiped the mud from Archie's paw and blotted his coat dry. Then the two of them went into the kitchen to see if there was anything suitable for a dog to eat.

She found an uneaten hamburger in the refrigerator. Emma broke it into pieces and set them in a bowl on the floor. As Archie dug in, she filled a second bowl with water and set it down, too. When he'd finished the burger and drunk his fill, Emma put him back on her lap and began carefully picking the brambles and goose grass from his coat.

"Boy, is Todd going to be happy to see you," she said. "He's been worried sick."

Emma glanced at the clock and bit her lip.

I wonder if I should call and tell him.

No, she thought, it'd be morning soon enough. Better to let Todd get some rest.

As happy as Emma was that Archie had been found, her joy was bittersweet. Having his dog back meant that Todd would be leaving in the morning. Who knew if she'd ever see him again? Still, she reminded herself, it wasn't her place to persuade him to stay.

When at last Archie's coat was clean, Emma set him down on a pillow, covered him with a blanket, and crawled back into bed. She'd been exhausted before; now she could barely move. She put her head on the pillow and had just begun to drift off when she heard a noise in the kitchen. Emma lifted her head and saw Archie, sitting in front of the open refrigerator door, surveying its contents. Had he opened it himself?

"Still hungry, huh?"

He glanced back at her and licked his chops.

Emma was too tired to argue.

"Okay," she said. "Just make sure you close the door when you're through."

CHAPTER 11

The telephone in Todd's room rang promptly at six. He rolled over and grabbed for the receiver twice before bringing it to his ear.

"Good morning," Emma said. "This is your wake-up call."

Todd shook his head. The phone had pulled him out of a dream; it took him a second to realize where he was.

"I didn't order a wake-up call," he grumbled, squinting at the clock.

"Oh. Well, since you're awake, why don't you come down to my cottage? I've got something I want to show you before I start work."

He yawned and rolled a kink out of his shoulder.

"Give me ten minutes," he said, and hung up.

Todd stepped out of the front door and shivered. When the rain left that morning, it had taken the cloud cover with it and the temperature had dropped noticeably. The puddles and tree branches were glazed with ice and the grass looked as sharp as knives. He thrust his hands into his pockets and started down the path toward Emma's cottage, his breath leaving a trail of white puffs in his wake. If he couldn't figure out how to open the suitcase soon, Todd thought, he'd have to find a store where he could buy some warmer clothing and heavier boots. He could already feel his toes getting numb.

What was it that Emma wanted him to see? And why was it so important that he come right then, before she started work? He smiled. Maybe there wasn't anything to show him. Maybe it was just an excuse for the two of them to be alone.

Since seeing Emma last night, he'd been thinking a lot about the summers they'd spent together as kids. She was Todd's first crush, the first girl he'd ever thought of as something other than a giggling, finicky annoyance. There'd been times in the past when he'd wondered if their feelings for each other had been blossoming into something more than a summer romance, but then he'd remind himself that it was foolish to dwell on what-ifs and put the thought aside. As the years passed, the question of whether or not he and Emma might have been falling in love became a moot point.

Todd felt a twinge of guilt as he realized how excited he was to be seeing Emma again. He and Gwen were together now; they were about to become engaged. Fantasizing about another woman was not only childish, it was disloyal. How would he feel if Gwen were off somewhere flirting with an old boyfriend? Whatever Emma had to show him, he was determined not to stay for long.

The cottage was in sight now, its whitewashed siding and periwinkle blue shutters a cheerful contrast to the wintry weather. Someone had removed the overgrown shrubs that had once shrouded the tiny structure and replaced them with a neat row of dwarf boxwood. Unless he missed his guess, there would be day lilies in the planting beds come springtime. The Spirit Inn might be an imposing Victorian mansion, but Emma's cottage looked like a cozy English dollhouse. He wiped his feet on the welcome mat and knocked.

Todd heard whispering inside, then quick, light footsteps. The door swung open.

"Surprise!" Emma said.

Before Todd could ask what the surprise was, Archie dashed through the doorway, jumping and barking, whirling like a dervish.

"Archie!" he cried.

He scooped up the little dog and hugged him gratefully. Archie was okay! He wasn't trapped; he wasn't starving; no bear or coyote had mauled him. Todd felt as if a weight had been lifted from his shoulders. It was like witnessing a miracle.

He buried his face in Archie's fur.

"Boy, you smell good," he said.

"That's baby shampoo," Emma told him. "I just finished blowing him dry."

Todd stared at her. "You did?"

"Come on in," she said, laughing. "I'll tell you all about it."

His first impression of the cottage as a dollhouse was reinforced when Todd stepped inside. He'd remembered the place being much larger, a maze of supplies and broken appliances that Emma's grandmother had used as the hotel's de facto storage shed, but which he, Claire, and Emma regarded as their personal clubhouse. What he'd thought of as a vast space was in fact a studio apartment with scaled-down appliances in its efficiency kitchen, a table for two, and a sleeper couch. Todd looked around at the modest, tasteful furnishings and felt pleased that his old friend—a rootless, unhappy orphan—had been able to create such a warm and inviting home for herself. He tried not to contrast it with the cold, avant-garde furnishings that Gwen had recently filled his own house with, reminding himself that it wasn't fair to compare the two, especially since his girlfriend wasn't there to defend herself.

"Archie showed up this morning around two," Emma said. "He was muddy and it looked like he'd rolled in every sticker bush on the property."

She picked a wicked-looking burr up off the table and handed it to Todd.

"This was stuck in his right front paw."

Todd stared at the sharp, yellowish spines, which were nearly an inch long.

"That's a spiny cocklebur seed," Emma said. "The plants are invasive around here. Livestock that eat those things get sick; some of them die."

"Poor guy."

"I picked the burrs out last night," she said, "and saved the bath for this morning."

Mud? Cockleburs? A bath? Todd was blown away. Gwen would never have done so much for an animal that wasn't hers, especially one that had interrupted her beauty sleep.

"Thank you," he said. "I can't tell you how much this means to me."

He set the burr aside and gave Archie a gentle shake.

"You had me worried, you little poop."

Emma smiled. "He ate pretty much everything I had in the fridge, but you'll need to get him some dog food before you go to Claire's. And don't blame me if the pizza gives him gas. It wasn't my idea."

Pizza?

Todd decided not to pursue it. Emma had saved his dog. If Archie turned into a stink bomb, at least he was still alive.

"Anyway," Emma said. "I checked with the weather service and the roads should be clear in another hour or so. I'm sure you'd like to get back on the road."

Todd felt his good mood evaporate. He'd been so glad to

have Archie back that he'd forgotten it meant there was nothing to stop him now from leaving. It felt as if he'd just arrived.
Did he really have to go so soon? Todd was in no hurry to get
rid of Archie, and he and Emma had barely had time to catch
up with each other. Besides, she'd washed his dog and comped
him a room for the night. Didn't he owe her something for
that?

"Maybe you'll let me do some chores around here to pay
you back before I go."

She raised an eyebrow. "I thought you had to get to
Claire's."

"Her place is only an hour away." He shrugged. "I'm not in
a hurry if you don't mind my hanging around awhile longer."

Emma shrugged.

"No, I don't mind. I'm sure my handyman, Jake, could find
something for you to do."

Todd glanced at his dog.

"Can Archie stay in here?"

Archie, who'd been happily panting as he listened to their
conversation, reeled in his tongue and cocked his head.

"It's fine with me," Emma said. "After the day he had yesterday, it might even be better if he got some more rest."

She pointed to the pillow and blanket she'd given Archie
the night before.

"He's welcome to hang out here until you're ready to go."

"Excellent," Todd said. "And in the meantime, I'll try to
make myself useful."

"Are you sure? You don't have to, you know."

Todd set Archie on the pillow and tucked the blanket
around him.

"I'm sure."

"All right," Emma said, grabbing her coat. "If you knock

on the back door and tell the kitchen staff I sent you, they'll give you some breakfast. I'll talk to Jake when he gets in."

Todd was about to tell her that he could pay for his own breakfast, but Emma was already halfway out the door.

"I'll see if we can get you some work clothes, too," she said. "Come by my office when you're ready to get started."

In the kitchen, Todd was treated to a farmhand's breakfast: pancakes, eggs, and hash brown potatoes filled one plate; a second was piled high with bacon and house-made sausage. Looking at all the food in front of him, Todd couldn't help thinking about the wheatgrass smoothies and egg-white omelets that Gwen swore were the keys to a long and healthy life.

Oh, well, he thought. *When in Rome . . .*

When he'd finished, he thanked the cook, handed his plates to the dishwasher, and went back to his room to call Gwen.

Five more rings and another message left on her voice mail. As Todd broke the connection, he began to wonder what Gwen was doing that she didn't have time to call him back. It wasn't like her not to return his calls. Then again, maybe her cell phone was out of range. Service out on the island could be pretty spotty.

He walked down to the lobby and saw Clifton at the front desk. The man gave him an unctuous smile.

"Good morning, Mr. Dwyer. May I help you?"

"Is Emma around?"

"Miss Carlisle is in a meeting," Clifton said. "As soon as she's free, I'll let her know you're here."

Todd looked around for a place to sit, but all the chairs were taken by people he assumed were there for the convention. They were a well-dressed bunch—even moneyed, perhaps— who nevertheless gave a strong impression of the counterculture. As they milled around, conversing with one another, the general mood of the room was one of excited anticipation. Whatever these ghost hunters had come looking for, it seemed that some of them, at least, had already found it.

After a few minutes spent wandering around the lobby, curiosity got the better of him and he approached a middle-aged couple who looked as if they might know what was going on.

"Excuse me," Todd said. "Are you here for the convention?"

"Indeed we are," the man said in a voice more suited for the theater than the inn's modest foyer.

He offered a slight bow.

"I'm Professor Lars Van Vandevander. This is my wife, Vivienne."

"Viv." The woman smiled. "Lars is one of the featured speakers."

"Oh. Congratulations."

Todd introduced himself and the two men shook hands.

"Are you a member of SSSPA?" the professor said.

"No," Todd said. "Just a guest, but I'm curious. What does 'spa' stand for?"

The Van Vandevanders glanced at each other and smiled.

"The Society for the Scientific Study of Paranormal Activity," the professor said.

Viv nodded. "We're ghost hunters."

"I see."

"Lars and I have been touring Washington's haunted places in preparation for his lecture tonight."

"A fascinating journey," the professor said. "New Mexico, of course, is touted as *the* state for encountering UPs—"

"Unexplained phenomena," Viv whispered.

"—but for my money, the Pacific Northwest has a far more interesting mix of both PA and EVP activity."

Todd nodded. "So, as far as you're concerned, this place is genuinely haunted?"

"It certainly is. It's on the NRHP."

"The N, R . . . ?"

"The National Register of Haunted Places."

The Van Vandevanders shared an anxious look.

"However, you mustn't worry," the professor said. "Most encounters are benign."

His wife nodded. "Poltergeists are notoriously shy."

"In fact," Lars continued, "there was one here just last night."

Todd looked nonplussed. "An encounter?"

"More of an auditory anomaly, really; a sort of piercing wail, or keening. Viv and I heard it, as did several of the other guests."

"When was that?"

Viv screwed up her face. "Oh, I don't remember. Do you, dear?"

Lars shook his head.

"Around midnight, perhaps? I'm afraid I didn't notice the time." He looked at Todd. "I'm sorry you missed it."

"I'm sorry, too," Todd said. "I stayed here several times as a kid and I don't remember ever encountering a ghost."

He glanced back at the front desk and saw Clifton waving him over.

"Looks like I have to go," he said. "It was nice meeting you both. Good luck with your lecture tonight."

"Perhaps you'd like to come," Viv said hopefully.

Todd shook his head. "I didn't pay for the conference. It wouldn't be fair."

"Oh, pish posh," the professor said. "I'm allowed a guest or two, and Viv would be thrilled. Wouldn't you, dear?"

His wife nodded. "I felt a strong harmonic resonance with you as soon as we met."

Todd pursed his lips thoughtfully.

"Let me think about it," he said.

"Good!" Lars said. "We'll be in the Energy Room. Viv will save a seat for you in the front row."

CHAPTER 12

Whatever mistakes Emma might have made in her love life, she prided herself on knowing they'd never interfered with her work. Of course Clifton, having been close to Gran, had been privy to some of the details, but even those had come to him only secondhand, and all of that had preceded Emma's inheritance of the inn.

A young woman in her position couldn't afford to let personal feelings undercut her authority. As far as her day-to-day dealings with the staff were concerned, she was scrupulously evenhanded, careful not to show any sort of favoritism. That was why, she supposed, this conversation with her handyman was so difficult. Jake had come in early that day, and when Emma called him into her office, he must have assumed she was ready to give him the funds for the roof. Instead, she'd asked him to give Todd a job.

As much as she might have protested that it wasn't permanent and that Todd wasn't even being paid, Emma had to admit that it looked bad. A handsome stranger from her past shows up at the inn and offers to work there for free? If she'd been in Jake's shoes, she'd have thought it sounded fishy, too.

"He's a little down on his luck at the moment," Emma

said. "But I'm sure he's a hard worker. Can't you find something for him to do?"

Jake crossed his arms and gave Emma a skeptical look. Only yesterday, he'd been telling her he needed help to fix the roof; it'd sound strange if he refused the assistance of an able-bodied workman. But Emma hadn't said anything about the loan coming through, and the rest of his projects could be done by one man alone. The look on his face said there had to be more behind her request than simply accommodating a friend.

"I already got the place ready for winter," he said. "Not much left to do around here 'cept fix the roof."

Emma nodded. It was pretty much what she'd expected him to say. Jake wasn't the sort to leave things to the last minute. Unless something extraordinary came up—like the roof repair—he could generally handle whatever maintenance the inn needed on his own. Still, she thought, there had to be some way to let Todd feel as if he'd earned his keep. The man might be down and out, but he still had his pride.

"What about the fence behind the cottage?" she said.

"I thought you said that could wait," Jake said. "Besides, I'll need lumber to shore it up."

"How much lumber?"

She was thinking about the balance in her bank account. If at least a few of the ghost hunters paid their bills in cash, she'd have enough to cover the cost of materials. And as soon as the bank approved her loan, she could breathe easy.

"Not sure," Jake said. "I'll have to inspect what's left of the old one, first. If we can salvage some of it, we might be able to save ourselves a bit of money."

"That's great! Tell you what: Why don't you and Todd take a look at the fence and see what it would take to fix it? Once you know how much you'll need, I'll give you a check to take to the lumberyard."

Emma smiled encouragingly as Jake shook his head. Before he could raise another objection, she stood and opened her office door.

"Let's go out and see if he's here," she said. "Once you meet Todd, I think you'll really like him."

Todd was standing in the lobby, talking to the Van Vandevanders. As he finished his conversation and walked toward the front desk, Emma felt her breath catch in her throat. What had happened to the geeky bespectacled kid she used to hunt crawdads with?

He wasn't just taller now; he was muscular in a way that suggested he spent a lot of time doing manual labor. Was it possible he was in construction? That would certainly explain the lack of steady work. It might also dispel some of the doubts that Jake had about hiring him.

Todd grinned at her and Emma had to struggle to keep from blushing.

"This is Jake, my handyman. He and I were just talking about how you might be able to give him a hand."

She turned toward the stony-faced Jake.

"This is Todd Dwyer. His family used to come to the inn when we were kids."

The two men looked like boxers in a ring as they shook hands. Emma felt her stomach tighten.

"Jake says he could use some help replacing the fence behind my cottage," she said. "I thought maybe you could go down there with him and see what it would take to get that done."

Todd smiled gamely. "Sounds good."

"First, however, I think you'll need some warmer clothes." She turned to Jake. "Don't we have some heavy jackets in the shop?"

He nodded. "Seems like there's gloves and a parka out there might fit him."

"Great. While you look for those, I'll see if we've got some better work clothes and a pair of boots in the Lost and Found."

As they headed down the hallway toward the back of the inn, Emma smiled.

"Don't let Jake scare you. He looks tough, but he's a softie inside."

"Thanks," Todd said. "I'll remember that."

They turned the corner and stopped at a door marked *Maintenance.*

"This is where we keep the things our guests leave behind. Honestly, some of the stuff would amaze you."

As she unlocked the door, Todd hesitated.

"I don't want to wear something that belongs to one of your guests."

Emma laughed. "Don't worry. Most of this stuff's been in here for years. I doubt anyone's going to come looking for it."

She pulled a bin off one of the shelves and removed the lid.

"This one's full of men's clothing, and I know there's at least two pairs of boots in it."

They began digging through the contents, Emma checking for sizes.

"Here's a wool shirt you can wear," she said. "By the way, how was breakfast?"

"Great," Todd said. "I don't remember the last time I ate that well."

In spite of herself, Emma felt disappointed. It was even worse than she'd feared. Todd was penniless.

"Aha!" he said, yanking a pair of Timberland boots from the jumble in the bin. He pulled up the tongue and smiled.

"Just my size, too. Mind if I try them on?"

"Go ahead."

While Todd tried on the boots, Emma drew out a pair of carpenter's pants and set them aside. Then she replaced the lid and slid the bin back onto the shelf.

"Those boots have been in there since before Gran died," she said. "If they fit, why don't you keep them?"

Todd finished tying the laces and stood, stamping his feet to loosen the stiff material.

"These are great," he said, beaming. "No more numb toes for me."

They went back out into the hallway and Emma locked the door.

"Now let's go see what Jake's got for you."

What Jake had was a pair of coveralls and a North Face parka that smelled like it'd been sitting in a compost pile. In spite of Emma's objections, Todd insisted upon wearing it. It smelled fine, he said, and thanked Jake for loaning it to him. From the look on her handyman's face, Emma guessed that it was not the reaction he'd been expecting. In spite of himself, Jake seemed to be developing a grudging respect for his new assistant.

Maybe, Emma thought, if Todd did really well, she'd consider hiring him to help Jake with the roof. Provided, of course, the bank approved her loan. Which it was going to, any day now.

The two men were about to step outside when Todd pulled up short.

"Oh," he said. "Before I forget, the Vander-somethings invited me to a lecture tonight."

Emma laughed. "It's Van Vandevander. Lars and Viv, right?"

"Right. Anyway, I'd kind of like to go, but it means I'd have to stay another night."

She felt her pulse quicken. Was it possible that Todd was as reluctant to go as she was to have him leave?

"Um, sure. If you want to."

"I'll pay for the room," he added quickly.

"No, that's okay."

Todd shook his head.

"I insist. I don't want to be a freeloader."

"All right," she said. "You can pay for the room."

He looked sheepish.

"There is one thing, though. You'd have to keep Archie another night."

"I'd be happy to. He was so quiet last night, I didn't even notice he was there."

As the two men trudged off toward her cottage, Emma smiled. She'd fallen for some lazy hunks before. Maybe it was time to fall for a hardworking one, instead.

CHAPTER 13

Jake might be a softie, Todd thought as he followed him down the path to the cottage, but he had a pretty tough exterior. From the second they'd met, the older man had been sizing him up, and Todd had a feeling he'd fallen short of whatever standard the handyman had been measuring him by. He didn't think it was jealousy, exactly, but there was something about Jake's demeanor that said he felt protective of his employer. Emma might be the boss, but she was still a woman, after all. Maybe Jake felt it was his job to keep her from being taken advantage of.

Todd, however, was used to having people underestimate him. He'd been small as a kid and something of a bookworm, reading science fiction at lunchtime and teaching himself computer code after he'd finished his chores at night. A late growth spurt had saved him from being the shortest boy in his senior class, but he'd been too busy working and taking care of his mom and Claire to capitalize on it.

The physical demands of maintaining his parents' house had had at least one positive side effect, though, as it compensated for the long hours he spent sitting in front of a computer screen, studying, or writing code. Now that he could afford to pay someone else to labor on his own home, Todd kept himself in shape at the gym, but he'd never forgotten how to frame a wall or repair a fence. Which was a good thing, because he had a feeling that Jake was going to make him sweat for that "free" hotel room.

Emma's cottage was in sight. As Todd glanced down the path, he saw the fallen remains of a fence he hadn't noticed before. It ran three-quarters of the way around the cottage and had fallen in sections, leaving the posts that had held it still in place. If he and Jake could pry the pickets off the broken rails without splitting them, they might not need more than a dozen two-by-fours to repair it.

"How long has it been down?" he asked Jake, as they drew closer.

"Since August," the handyman said. "Blew down in a storm."

"Too bad," Todd said, bending down to inspect a dilapidated section. "Some of these pickets look like they've got termite damage."

Jake grunted. "Some, yes, but not most. We'll remove the worst ones and treat the rest."

The two men lifted the section in question and Todd was relieved to see that the damage was not as bad as he'd feared.

"You treated these with borate?"

The handyman looked up, surprised.

"It's tough trying to stay green with all the rain we get up here," Todd said, "but it beats having arsenic leach into your groundwater, doesn't it?"

Again, Jake said nothing, but the look he gave Todd told him the comment had earned him some grudging respect.

The handyman had just begun calculating the amount of

lumber they'd need when Todd caught a flash of white in his peripheral vision. Turning, he saw Archie trot across the yard carrying something in his mouth.

What the heck?

"I'll be right back," he told Jake, and marched off to see what was going on.

Archie was on the far side of the cottage, hunkered beneath a bush and enjoying what appeared to be a sandwich. As Todd approached, the little dog started wolfing down the remainder.

"What have you got there?"

He squatted down to take a closer look and Archie gulped down the last few bites of his prize, sniffing the ground to make sure he hadn't missed anything.

"Looks like the kitchen staff's been feeding both of us pretty well," Todd said.

Archie sprang from his sanctuary and began covering Todd with grateful bacon-scented kisses.

"I guess I don't have to ask what kind of sandwich it was," he said. "Better enjoy it while you can, though. I have a feeling you won't be getting any BLTs from Bob and Claire."

The thought that he would soon be giving Archie away felt like a stab to Todd's heart. Not only because he'd grown fond of the little guy, but also because he'd be turning him over to people who viewed dogs differently from the way he did. Living with Bertie, Archie had been a partner and a friend—the same way that Todd thought of him—but at Bob and Claire's, he'd be an animal whose feelings were ignored, when they were considered at all. The boys might play with him for a while, but sooner or later they'd take their father's lead and leave the little dog to fend for himself. As much as his sister had said she wanted their uncle's dog, Todd knew that

Archie would be viewed as an obligation more than anything else.

He heard footsteps behind him.

"I'm finished here," Jake said. "Time to give Miss Emma the bad news."

"Just a minute," Todd said. "I want to put this guy back in the cottage."

He grabbed Archie's collar and walked him to Emma's front door. When the little dog was safely back inside and on his pillow bed, Todd closed the door firmly, testing it to make sure it couldn't open on its own. Archie might not be so quick to come back if he escaped a second time.

As the two men headed back up the path to the inn, Todd sensed a change in Jake's mood. For a while, it had seemed as if the two of them were establishing a friendly rapport. Now the man was no longer willing to engage in even a few words of conversation. Todd wondered what had prompted the switch. Was it something to do with the job? Perhaps Jake had been hoping there'd be more work for them to do. As puzzling as the change was, however, Todd wasn't about to mention it. Jake seemed like the sort of person who preferred to keep things to himself.

Emma was in the lobby when they returned with their estimate. Todd hung back and let Jake present her with his list of materials, feeling it wasn't his place to be involving himself in their deliberations. He was still painfully aware of Jake's protective attitude toward Emma. By hanging back, he hoped to show the older man that he wasn't interested in encroaching on their relationship.

Jake and Emma finished their discussion and she went back to her office, emerging a few seconds later with a check in her hand. Jake gave it a dubious look before folding it in half and tucking it into his wallet. Then he turned and headed for the front door, saying nothing to Todd as the two men walked out and got into Emma's truck.

Jake put his key in the ignition but didn't turn the engine over. Instead, he sat and stared at the dashboard. It seemed like such an obvious invitation to talk that Todd decided to risk it.

"Something wrong?" he said.

The handyman nodded.

"I don't like being sent on a fool's errand."

Todd frowned. They were going to the hardware store for lumber. It didn't sound foolish to him.

"What's the problem?"

"She gave me a check." Jake's look remained inscrutable. "The last one bounced."

"Oh," Todd said. "Well, one bounced check—"

"And the one before that, and another one about six months ago. Last time I was down there, they told me the inn would have to be cash only from now on."

Todd was stunned. He'd assumed that Emma was flush, that the inn was making money and that she was doing well. Now it seemed as if that assumption was wrong.

"I take it you didn't tell her?"

Jake shook his head. "Didn't have the heart."

Here was the softie Emma knew, Todd thought. The handyman who shielded her from bad news and protected her from heartbreakers. No wonder Jake looked crestfallen. He'd run out of options.

"Why don't I take the check and see if they'll let me pay?" he said.

"What difference would that make?"

"Well, they told you no more checks, but they didn't tell me, right? Maybe if I just hand it over, the clerk will accept it. It's good this time, right?"

Jake nodded. "She swore to me it was."

"Then it's no problem," Todd said. "We'll get the things we need, and when it's time to pay, you head out to the truck and wait. I'll give the clerk the check and see what happens."

The older man thought about that for a second.

"No," he said, shaking his head. "It won't work."

"Maybe not," Todd said. "But it's worth a try, isn't it? People tell me I'm pretty persuasive."

The comment earned him a deeply skeptical look, but no argument. Jake started up the truck and put it in gear.

"Fine," he grumbled. "But when we come back empty-handed, you'll have to be the one to tell her."

The trip into town was an eye-opener. Jake's revelation about the bounced checks had apparently breached a dam that had been holding back a flood of concerns, and as he drove he shared them freely with Todd.

The Spirit Inn was faltering, he said. Business wasn't bad, but even at the busiest times, its profits were elusive. Neither Emma nor Clifton could figure out what the problem was, but if they didn't discover it soon, the place would go under. Even the loan she was counting on might not be enough to keep Emma from having to sell the place. By the time they pulled into the hardware store's parking lot, Todd was worried. After all her hard work, it was sad to think his old friend might lose it all.

Talking about the inn's imminent demise had had the opposite effect on Jake, however. Being able to unburden himself to someone must have been cathartic, Todd thought. As they walked through the lumberyard, checking the two-by-fours and loading them onto their utility cart, the handyman whistled. Maybe the thought of having someone else try to deal with the manager for once had lightened his mood.

When everything they needed had been gathered, Jake handed over the check and headed out the door.

"I'll be waiting in the truck," he said. "Don't say I didn't warn you."

Todd waited until he was sure Jake was gone before pushing their supplies up to the counter. As the cashier totaled his order, he fingered the check, wondering what she'd say when he presented it. Was Jake right? He hoped not. Todd wished with all his might that Emma's situation was not as dire as it seemed and that her check would be accepted without question. But Todd was a businessman, and he knew that no one who accepted bad checks could stay afloat for long.

When the cashier finished ringing up his order, he filled in the amount on the check and handed it over. The woman glanced at the business name on the front and back up at Todd before calling for the manager.

"I'm sorry," the man said. "I thought Miss Carlisle understood."

"Of course," Todd said.

As hard as it was for him to have the truth confirmed, he could tell that it was hard for the manager, too. In a small town, where everyone knew everyone else's business, one person's misfortune was felt by all.

"It's nothing personal. We just can't afford to keep chasing after bad paper."

"No, I understand perfectly. You don't need to explain."

"I'm glad you do," the manager said, looking relieved. "The fact is, we simply can't take the risk."

"Of course not," Todd said.

Then he reached into his back pocket, removed his wallet, and took out his own platinum MasterCard. As he set it down on the counter, the manager's eyes bulged. Todd gave him a wry smile.

"But you will accept this, won't you?"

The truck was idling at the curb when Todd walked out. No doubt Jake had been ready to beat a hasty retreat when his employer's old friend left the store empty-handed. Instead, the handyman's mouth hung open as he watched the manager help Todd carry their supplies across the sidewalk and load them into the back of his truck. Todd thanked the man for his assistance and got back into the cab.

"I don't believe it," Jake said. "How in the hell did you manage that?"

Todd gave him a confident shrug.

"I told you. I'm pretty persuasive."

CHAPTER 14

While Todd and Jake were at the hardware store, Emma spent some time visiting with her guests. The ghost hunters were still buzzing about the so-called encounter of the night before, and the more the tale was retold, the more fantastic it became. The brief series of moans was now described as the cry of a banshee, and the number of people claiming they'd heard it had grown from a handful to almost the entire SSSPA.

As a result, some of the "civilian" guests were beginning to look rattled, and Emma was careful to reassure them that whatever might—or might not—have occurred, it posed no danger to them. The ghost hunters might be good customers, after all, but they were by no means her only customers. The last thing she needed was to have a riot on her hands.

At least the spirits' reappearance had improved Viv Van Vandevander's mood. No longer unsure of her powers, she was once again in the thick of things, enjoying the notoriety of being the only true medium of the group, answering questions from the conventioneers, and deferring to Lars when historic details were required. As Emma watched the two of them hold court in the lobby, she smiled. They were good people, she thought, even if she didn't believe a word of what they were saying.

She was just heading back to the office when she heard her name being called. Emma turned in time to see Viv break away from her acolytes and come hurrying in her direction, *suzu* bells jingling, her billowing skirt making it seem as if she was floating on air. Viv clutched Emma's arm and spun her around as the two of them scurried out of earshot.

"Emma, dear," she purred. "Who was that delicious young man we saw you with?"

It took a moment for Emma to realize that the "delicious young man" Viv was referring to was Todd.

"Oh," she said. "That's just Todd. He's an old friend."

Viv's eyes were twinkling.

"Well, he seemed quite taken with you. I believe I saw sparks flying as he watched you talking to your handyman."

Emma felt her cheeks redden. Was it true? she wondered. She'd certainly felt some sparks of her own when she saw Todd in the lobby, but it hadn't occurred to her that he might feel the same. She tried to keep her imagination under control, but it wasn't easy with Viv practically panting for news.

"We were sweet on each other when we were kids, I guess," she said. "But I haven't seen him in years. The only reason he's here is because his dog ran away. I offered to let him stay until he found it."

"And did he?"

"Yes."

Viv gave her a knowing look.

"Yet he's still here. I wonder why?"

This was ridiculous, Emma told herself. The fact that Todd Dwyer had wandered into the Spirit Inn the day before was an accident. It had had nothing to do with her or what ei-

ther of them had meant to each other in the past. It was
Archie's doing, not hers.

Still, Viv was having none of it.

"He's coming to Lars's lecture tonight—did he tell you
that?"

"Yes. He said you'd invited him. That was very nice."

"It was a calculated move on my part," Viv said. "He has
one of the most glorious auras I've ever seen. Men of great
wealth often do, you know."

Emma could barely keep from smirking. Great wealth?
Well, that settled any question she might have had about Viv's
so-called abilities. If she thought a guy who couldn't afford a
change of clothing and a decent meal had a glorious aura, then
the great Vivienne Van Vandevander needed to get her eyes
checked.

Still, there was no need to be rude about it.

"That's interesting," Emma said. "Thanks for the information."

Viv seemed puzzled.

"Of course, I'm sure you want to make up your own mind
about him," she said. "But to the extent that you might find it
helpful, I thought I'd give you my professional opinion. Don't
string him along forever, though, my dear. He's definitely a
keeper."

With that, she turned and floated back to the lobby. Emma
suppressed a giggle.

Great wealth, indeed. Todd would be laughing out loud.

Of course, just because Viv was wrong about Todd's material circumstances didn't mean she was wrong about the way
he felt about Emma. It was a whole lot easier to read someone's
face and body language, after all, than it was to read something
as insubstantial as an aura. Maybe she wasn't the only one who
still remembered their summers fondly, Emma thought. Maybe

Todd, too, wished the two of them could rekindle their once-budding romance.

It seemed like another good omen. First Archie, then the sparks. People said good news came in threes, didn't they? Maybe her loan approval would be next.

As Emma headed back to her office, she thought about the work that needed to be done on the roof. She hoped that Todd and Jake were getting along. If so, maybe she'd ask Todd to stay so he and Jake could fix the roof together. He needed a job, after all, and it'd be a big help to have someone on hand who'd work for room and board, at least temporarily.

If Todd agreed, then Emma could give him the sort of leg up that her Gran had given her. He could turn his life around, have another chance to be a success in life. Emma smiled and bit her lip. Now that she thought of it, there were a lot of things around the inn that Todd might be able to fix.

Thinking about things around the inn reminded Emma that she hadn't checked on Archie in a while. If she took a detour through the back, she figured she could make it down to her cottage and back before Todd and Jake returned. With breakfast over, the kitchen would no longer be the hive of activity that it had been since dawn and there'd be no chance of upsetting Jean-Paul by cutting through his domain. She turned and walked back down the hall.

The stainless steel counters had been scrubbed clean and the pots and pans returned to their places on the shelves. When Emma opened the door, the only staff in sight was the prep cook, a middle-aged man with more tattoos than hair, who was laying out the salad greens for lunch. As she stepped into the room, though, all hell broke loose.

"Hey, what happened to my lunch?"

She heard rapid footsteps and saw her dishwasher emerge from the pantry, his face red with indignation. The sandy-haired teenager stormed over to the back door and yanked it open, admitting a blast of cold air that ruffled the aprons hanging on the wall. One of the busboys was on the landing outside, slouched against the handrail, smoking a cigarette.

"Give it back!" the dishwasher said.

The busboy blew out a lungful of smoke.

"Give what back?"

"My BLT."

"Don't look at me," the young man said, tossing his cigarette aside. "I didn't take it."

The dishwasher stepped forward, put his hands against the busboy's chest, and shoved. The young man gave a shout of surprise and toppled over backward.

Emma ran for the door, followed closely by the prep cook, but before either one could stop him, the dishwasher had launched himself over the railing.

The young men were grappling on the ground, ice and mud flying in all directions. The prep cook charged past Emma, swearing at the young men, then pulled them to their feet and held them by their shirt collars. When they saw her standing there, the two of them looked shamefaced.

"What was that all about?" she demanded.

The dishwasher pointed an accusatory finger.

"He took my sandwich. I left it in the pantry and now it's gone."

"I did not," the busboy said. "Why would I take your stupid sandwich, anyway? I don't take my lunch break until two."

"He told me it looked good," the youth pleaded. "He's always doing stuff like that."

Emma stood there, arms akimbo, and gave the busboy a severe look.

"Did you take his sandwich?"

"No," he said firmly.

She looked at the prep cook.

"Did you see him take the sandwich?"

The older man shook his head.

"I wasn't watching, but I'm pretty sure I'd have heard him if he did."

Emma looked back at the dishwasher.

"And you're sure you left it in the pantry?"

He nodded, his chin trembling.

She stood glaring at the two young men, both of them mud-covered, both aggrieved, and considered her options.

"Sandwiches don't just disappear," she said. "If nobody took it, then what happened to it?"

As the three of them exchanged a worried glance, the intercom squawked. There was a call for Emma on line one. She shook her head in frustration.

"I'll figure out what to do about this later," she said. "In the meantime, the two of you get cleaned up. And if I hear about anyone fighting again, I won't hesitate to fire them. Understood?"

When Emma saw the bank's phone number on her caller ID, she felt breathless. She hadn't realized how keyed up she'd been about the loan until then, and it made her laugh out loud that the suspense was finally over. As she hit the button for the speakerphone, she felt grateful that the loan committee hadn't made her wait through the weekend. She'd have to be sure to thank Harold Grader for agreeing to resubmit her request.

"Emma speaking."

"Hi, Emma, it's Harold Grader. Sorry to bother you on a weekend, but I wanted to call as soon as the loan committee made their decision."

A bother? she thought. With a leaking roof to fix, delayed maintenance to catch up on, and improvements she hoped would increase the inn's cash flow, this call was literally the answer to her prayers.

"I'll make this short," he said. "The loan committee's turned you down."

She felt her body begin to shake. *No*, she thought. This had to be a mistake. It couldn't be right.

"I see." Her voice was thick with emotion. "Well, I'm sure you tried your best. Thank you for letting me know."

"I'm afraid it's worse than that," he said.

Worse? Wasn't turning her down bad enough? How much worse could it get?

"The committee members are concerned about the loan you have presently. You've—well, we discussed this already—you've only been paying the minimum each month, and not always on time."

Emma's heart was pounding. "What are you saying?"

The banker sighed and for just a moment she imagined how difficult this call had been for him to make. Then a surge of anger wiped out any sympathy she might have felt. *This is my whole life*, she thought. *To him, it's just business as usual.*

"We're calling in your loan," he said. "The bank will expect full repayment by the end of this month."

The effect of his words on Emma was like a blow to the head. Her ears rang; she felt dizzy and disoriented; the ground beneath her felt as if it were crumbling to dust. She fought to keep her voice steady.

"Thank you for letting me know."

Emma hung up and buried her head in her hands. This was the end of everything. Without that loan, the roof wouldn't make it through the holidays; she'd have to close the banquet and conference rooms at the height of ski season. Half their bookings—maybe more—would be canceled overnight, and the income she'd counted on to get her through the leaner months would disappear. Everything she had, everything she'd hoped for, would be gone.

"I'm sorry, Gran," she whispered as tears spilled down her cheeks. "I guess I really let you down."

There was a knock on the door. Emma sat up and quickly wiped her eyes.

"Come in."

Clifton stepped into the room and closed the door behind him.

"That was the bank?"

Emma nodded, afraid that if she said anything she'd start crying again.

"I take it they rejected your application."

She cleared her throat. Clifton had been working there since her grandmother bought the place. He deserved to know the truth.

"They called my loan in, too," she said. "I've got until the end of the month to pay it off."

"I'm sorry to hear that," he said.

"Don't tell the staff yet, okay? I'd rather they heard it from me."

He nodded. "Of course."

"And I don't want the conventioneers to get wind of this, either. We've got two more bookings from their affiliates coming up. I'd rather not lose those if we don't have to."

"I won't say a word."

When Clifton had gone, Emma stood. She had to get out of there. She needed to think, but most important, she needed to be somewhere where her tears wouldn't be seen by the staff or the guests. She'd have to come up with a plan, of course, but first Emma would have to give vent to her pain and sadness. If only there was someone she could unburden herself to without worrying they'd panic or leave, she thought. A confidant who would listen patiently without jumping in with a solution before she'd had a chance to come up with one of her own.

Archie.

In spite of her situation, the realization almost made her smile. She closed up her office and hurried down to the cottage.

CHAPTER 15

Todd's success at the hardware store had gone far beyond merely lifting Jake's spirits; as they drove back to the inn, the man was practically giddy about their improved fortunes. For Todd, however, the solution to one problem had just created two more.

Sooner or later, he'd have to give the uncashed check back to Emma and the bitter truth that her handyman had been reluctant to share would be his to deliver. Todd didn't know how bad the inn's financial situation was, but the fact that he knew there was a problem would be an embarrassment to Emma. It also made it hard to tell her about his own circumstances.

Unlike a lot of guys who'd made it big, Todd hadn't forgotten what it was like to come from modest means, and he knew that sometimes the friends who'd cheered you on as you struggled found it hard to be supportive once you'd made it. Todd didn't want the knowledge of his newly acquired wealth to affect their relationship.

Still, he wasn't sorry for what he'd done. Not only because it had brightened Jake's gloomy mood, but also because it meant that the two of them had the materials needed to fix

Emma's fence. It was the least he could do to pay her back for all she'd done for him.

As they turned off the main road and headed toward the inn, Jake cleared his throat.

"You have a lot of experience with construction?"

"Some," Todd said. "My dad died when I was a kid, and maintaining the house pretty much fell to me. I'd helped him enough on the weekends that I knew the basics, and when I had a big project a neighbor let me use his power tools. Most of what I learned was through trial and error."

Jake considered that awhile.

"Ever done any roofing?"

"Sure," Todd said. "I reroofed our entire house the summer between my sophomore and junior years in college."

As the grade grew steeper, the weight of the materials in back made the truck's engine labor. Jake downshifted and glanced at Todd thoughtfully.

"The inn's roof needs shoring up," he said. "If you're looking for a job, I could use an experienced hand."

The offer had come out of left field, and Todd wasn't sure how to answer.

"It's flattering to think you could use me," he said. "But I doubt I'm the person you need."

The handyman shrugged.

"Well, think about it. Miss Emma doesn't pay much, but she's a good employer. You might just find you'd like it around here."

The comment was puzzling. Up until then, Jake's attitude toward him had been standoffish in general and almost hostile where the subject of Emma was concerned. The older man had seemed more like her protective older brother than merely an employee. Why the change of heart? Once again, Todd had the feeling that he'd passed some sort of unspoken test.

They pulled into the parking lot and began unloading the truck, carrying the lumber and materials around to the side yard where Jake had his workshop. When everything had been put away, the handyman stood and stretched.

"Thought I'd head over to the kitchen before we get started. Can't do much on an empty stomach. You coming?"

Todd shook his head. The fact was, he hadn't done all that much since getting up that morning and he was still full from breakfast.

"Maybe later," he said. "I gotta go check on my dog."

When he reached the cottage, Todd hesitated. There was someone inside. As he stood there listening, he felt a growing concern. It sounded like whoever was in there was crying, and unless he missed his guess, it was Emma. He lifted his hand and gently knocked on the door.

Todd heard scuffling and a few words too quiet for him to make out. A few seconds later, the door swung open.

Emma's face was dry, but her eyes were puffy and her nose red. She'd kicked off her shoes and the front of her jacket was covered in dog fur. Archie stood beside her, looking up anxiously.

"Sorry," Todd said. "I just came by to see how Archie's doing."

"Thanks," she said. Her chin began to quiver.

Todd reached out. "Emma, what's wrong?"

She swiped angrily at a wayward tear that ran down her cheek.

"Nothing."

He gave her a knowing smile.

"You know, you used to tell me that nothing made you cry. Guess I should have believed you."

Emma spluttered, laughter bubbling up in spite of her tears.

Todd looked around. "Mind if I come in?"

She shook her head and stepped away from the door. Todd took a minute to dust off his clothes and remove his dirty boots. When he stepped inside, he found Emma and Archie on the couch, the little dog's head resting comfortably on her lap. He pulled up a chair and sat down.

"You want to tell me what's going on?"

Emma said nothing as she wiped away a tear and began stroking Archie's head. In Todd's experience, people didn't change much as they got older, and Emma had been a stubborn kid. She would talk to him or she wouldn't; trying to pry it out of her would be a waste of time.

After a few minutes of hesitant silence, she sighed.

"I'm going to lose this place."

He nodded and said nothing. After what Jake had told him, the news didn't come as a big surprise.

"It's been slowly going under ever since Gran died. I've done everything I could think of to bring in more business, but we're still bleeding money. I thought a loan might buy me some more time, but the bank just called . . ."

"I take it they turned you down."

"Not just that. They called in my other loan, too. I've got 'til the end of the month to pay it off." Emma smiled ruefully. "Sucks to be me, huh?"

Her lips began to tremble. She put her head down and great gulping sobs wracked her body.

"Oh, Emma. I'm so sorry."

This would be a bad situation for anyone, Todd thought, but it had to be especially difficult for her. Emma's Gran had been the one steady thing in her life; losing something they'd loved and worked on together had to be devastating.

Unless he missed his guess, the Spirit Inn was all she had in the world, too. By the time Emma sold it and settled up with the bank, she might not have enough to start over. With no family and a bad credit history, she'd have a hard time getting back on her feet.

His first impulse was to give her the money and let her pay him back when she could. Todd could afford to be generous, after all, and it would be a simple solution to her problem. But the more he thought about it, the less he liked the idea. Emma's problems weren't the result of a single catastrophic event. According to Jake, the Spirit Inn had been struggling ever since her grandmother died. If Emma didn't change the way she was running the place, it wouldn't matter that Todd had paid her loans off. Sooner or later, she'd find herself in the exact same position. If he was truly going to help her, he'd have to do more than just offer her money.

"If you don't mind my asking, what did you need the loans for?" he said.

Emma sniffed and sat back.

"Originally, I'd planned to use it all for upgrades like putting in a coffee bar, but we're behind on some of the maintenance around here and Jake just told me the roof needs to be repaired, so I guess most of it would have gone to that."

"Don't you have a rainy-day fund?" he said. "A place like this shouldn't have to borrow to cover its maintenance costs."

She frowned slightly but said nothing. Taking her silence as encouragement, Todd continued.

"Maybe instead of upgrading the inn, you should try to make it less expensive to run," he said. "The Victorian stuff is nice, but families aren't going to want to bring their kids here, and you said yourself that you don't like the haunted theme. Why risk scaring away potential customers when you could easily change the theme to something less expensive to maintain?"

Emma's face began to cloud over. She lifted Archie from her lap and set him aside.

"I'm sorry. I don't think that's any of your business."

Todd was surprised. He'd thought he was helping. Now it seemed as if he'd upset her.

"No, I suppose it isn't," he said. "But you seem to have gotten yourself into a bind and I thought you could use some advice."

"From *you?*"

He felt his lips tighten. Todd and his partners had spent the last five years building their company from nothing into a billion-dollar enterprise. He wasn't used to having people question his business savvy. But of course, Emma didn't know that, and this wasn't the time to tell her, either.

"Look, I'm sorry if I upset you," he said. "I'll admit I don't have a lot of experience with hotels, but I do know something about how a business should be run. If you don't like the way things are going, you've got to be open to change."

Emma got to her feet. Archie scrambled down and stood beside her.

"I am open to change," she said. "That's why I bought into the whole Victorian haunted-house thing in the first place. I told you, I can't compete with the chains up here. The Spirit Inn has to be a destination. Someplace people are willing to go out of their way for. Besides," she added, "it's too late to change anything now."

"But you're not happy the way things are. Why stay in a relationship that you know isn't working?"

He paused, frowning. *Why did I say that?*

"Look, I know you're just trying to help," Emma said, "but I think I have a little more business experience than you do, and I'd really rather work this out on my own."

"You're right," he said. "Forget I said anything."

He stood and headed for the door.

CHAPTER 16

When the door closed, Emma burst into a fresh flood of tears. Why did everyone think they could do her job better than she could? Her assistant manager, her banker, and now Todd had all felt free to weigh in on what she should be doing to save the inn. Did it never occur to them that she had a brain of her own?

Clifton and Mr. Grader she could understand; at least they knew something about her situation, but Todd had a lot of nerve. The guy was practically homeless and yet he'd sat there spouting advice as if she was the one who was barely getting by. What was it about her that made everyone think she was inept?

Archie trotted after her as she walked into the bathroom. No, Emma thought as she blew her nose, that wasn't fair. The fact was, she did need help; it was herself she was mad at. Todd might not be a businessman, but he meant well and all he'd really done was remind her of some things she already knew but was choosing to ignore. The Victorian theme *was* costing her a lot, and calling the Spirit Inn a haunted hotel was probably keeping away at least as many customers as it attracted. But what else could she do? Even if she'd had another theme in mind—

which she didn't—changing things would take time, and without the ghost hunters' business to keep her going, she wouldn't have enough income to hold out. Emma was stuck with things the way they were, whether she liked it or not.

A soft whimper brought her back from the gloom. She looked down and saw Archie turn and run out. Curious, Emma followed him back to the living room and watched as the little dog hopped onto his pillow bed and dove under the blanket she'd given him that morning. Seconds later, he poked his nose out and quickly ducked back under, then did it twice more. He was playing hide-and-seek, Emma realized. Even with all that had happened, she couldn't help smiling at Archie's attempt to cheer her up.

"I see you, you little ghost," she said.

Emma snatched the blanket away and scooped him up into her arms. Archie wriggled happily and began licking away the salty tracks on her cheeks, making her laugh in spite of herself.

"I wouldn't have to worry about losing customers," she said, "if all the ghosts around here were as sweet as you are."

She shook out the blanket and saw the places where Archie had gotten pizza sauce on it.

"Uh-oh," Emma said. "We'd better stick this in the hamper."

Archie followed her into the bathroom and watched forlornly as Emma tossed his blanket in with the rest of her dirty linens.

"Don't worry. Housekeeping will have it back by tonight. In the meantime," she said, opening a cabinet, "how about a nice towel?"

Emma took out a fresh pink bath towel and laid it on Archie's bed. The little dog sniffed it disdainfully and pushed it aside.

"I'm sorry, Your Majesty," she said. "But it's the best I can do."

With the temporary distraction over, Emma's smile began to fade. She didn't have a lot of time, she thought. If the bank wanted its money by the end of the month, she'd have to scramble to find another lender. Chances were, she could find someone, but the interest rate she'd be paying would leave her even deeper in the hole.

Still, this wasn't the time to be worrying about it. There was nothing she could do until tomorrow, and the ghost hunters were expecting a good time until then. She washed her face, brushed the fur off her jacket, and headed out the door.

Back at the inn, the ghost hunters were all atwitter. Several more encounters had been reported, including the unexplained "disappearance" of her dishwasher's sandwich. Emma was tempted to nip that one in the bud but told herself that it was no more fanciful than any of the other sightings the SSSPA was exulting over. After all, it was what they'd all come for. Where was the harm? Once the conventioneers were gone, there'd be plenty of time for her to have a word with the staff about the dangers of spreading rumors.

The Van Vandevanders had to be over the moon about the increased sightings, she thought. As Lars was in charge of that year's confab, the fact that it was turning out to be one of their most successful was not lost on anyone—especially his rival, Dr. Richards. While the rest of the group exchanged stories of the encounters thus far, the man roamed through the inn wearing a black look.

Adam looked up and smiled as Emma passed the front desk.

"Professor Van Vandevander was just looking for you."

"Oh?" Emma glanced around the lobby. "What did he want?"

"I'm not sure, but he said he'd be in the Spirit Room."

As she headed down to see what Lars wanted, Emma kept an eye out for Todd. He and Jake had been working on the fence for some time now and she wondered how it was going. She hoped their disagreement hadn't changed his mind about staying. How would she break it to Viv that she'd been responsible for chasing the "delicious young man" away?

She found the Van Vandevanders in the hall outside the Spirit Room, in consultation with three other members of their group, one of them Dr. Richards. As she approached, Richards was shaking his head vigorously. From the looks on the others' faces, his was the lone voice of opposition to some well-laid plan. What was going on?

"Ah, there she is," Lars crowed when he spied her.

Dr. Richards turned and glared.

"I'm sorry," Emma said. "I didn't mean to interrupt."

"Nonsense," Lars said. "Dick was just concluding his remarks."

He looked around at the others.

"The steering committee was just discussing the addition of a séance to tonight's program, and we need your buy-in to proceed."

Emma was taken aback.

"A séance?"

"A meeting in which a medium attempts to communicate with the departed," Viv said.

"Yes, I know what a séance is," she said. "I'm just not sure—"

"Precisely my point," Richards said brusquely. "We can't be sure. Which is why I believe that, under the present circumstances, any attempt at necromancy would be ill advised."

Viv arched an eyebrow.

"Providing the spirits with a link to the living hardly qualifies as a black art."

"Really?" he sneered. "What would you call it?"

Emma held up her hands. "Wait a minute. What are we talking about here? Are you saying that séances are dangerous?"

"Of course not," Viv scoffed.

"Dr. Richards is merely suggesting an abundance of caution," Lars added as the others nodded their agreement.

Richards seemed unconvinced.

"Is that true?" Emma asked him.

He shrugged unhappily as the rest of the committee pursed their lips.

"Perhaps," he mused. "Where the spirits are concerned, nothing is absolute."

She looked at the others.

"When would you be holding this séance?"

"Tonight," Lars said. "As a supplement to my lecture on the unexplained phenomena of the Pacific Northwest."

Emma considered that. From her point of view, the problem wasn't that a séance might endanger anyone. The issue for her was whether or not the séance would necessitate the use of another room. The only one available was the Spirit Room, and after her talk with Jake about the damaged roof, she felt uneasy about putting anyone in there.

"Are you asking for my permission?"

"Not for the séance," he said. "Not technically, anyway. What we need is your permission to move the venue from the Energy Room to the Spirit Room. Viv feels the vibrations here are more advantageous for a summoning."

It was exactly what Emma did not want to do, yet she felt unable to say no. Without some clear indication of structural damage, there was no reason to think that the ceiling in the Spirit Room was unsound. Then again, if she allowed the séance to be conducted in there and anything went wrong, she'd be in trouble.

Suddenly, Emma felt an overwhelming sense of fatigue.

Séances? Necromancy? Unexplained phenomena? None of it made any sense to her. Even worse, she realized that she didn't want it to make any sense. It was hard enough trying to run an inn, but the added layer of mystery and speculation involved in running a haunted one was a burden she felt increasingly unable to deal with. Maybe Todd was right; she wasn't happy with the way things were. But what else could she do?

The steering committee members were looking at her expectantly; she had to make a decision. She hated being pressured like this. Gran had always warned her not to make snap decisions.

"Let me think about it," she said. "Maybe we could have it in another room instead."

Lars looked at the others, who simply shook their heads. Viv shrugged.

"All right," he said. "Perhaps another venue would work as well. But do consider it, please."

"I will," Emma said. "I just need to make sure it's safe first, that's all."

The confrontation had left Emma feeling exhausted. In addition to everything else on her plate, she'd have to talk to Jake and ask him what he thought the actual risks might be. Whatever happened, she hoped she wouldn't be sorry.

But sorry was exactly what Emma was as she walked away. Sorry that she hadn't listened to Todd, sorry that she'd been so rude to him when all he'd done was point out what she already knew, and sorry that he might leave before she could tell him she'd been wrong to criticize his advice. She'd just have to apologize and hope he understood.

Jake was emerging from his toolshed when Emma stepped around the side yard.

"Come to see your new fence?" he said.

"Is it finished already?"

"It sure is. That assistant you got me knows more than he lets on. Come on," Jake said. "I'll show you."

As Emma followed him down toward the cottage, she saw the rebuilt fence. The new lumber would need a coat of paint to match the rest, but other than that, it looked as good as new.

"It's beautiful," she said.

"That Todd's a good worker," Jake said. "If he's still here when your loan comes through, I wouldn't mind having him help me with the roof."

Emma felt a pang. There wasn't going to be any loan, not right away, at least, and maybe not ever. She'd have to tell Jake sooner or later, but she didn't want to spoil his good mood just yet.

"I doubt Todd will be staying here that long," she said. "But when the time comes, we'll make sure you get a good assistant."

He considered that a moment.

"Maybe he would stay, if you asked him to." Jake looked at the tools in his hand. "I may not be an educated man, but I know love when I see it."

"I'm not sure you're right about that, but if he's not too proud to take it, I'm pretty sure he could use a job."

"Well, it's your decision, not mine."

Emma looked back toward the inn. Suddenly, asking Jake about the Spirit Room seemed like the wrong thing to do. He was right; she was the one who was supposed to make the decisions around here. Why was she always so unsure of herself?

If the Van Vandevanders wanted to hold a séance, that was fine, but they'd have to do it where Emma told them to. She couldn't keep making bad decisions because she was afraid of losing their business.

"I'd better go in. Are you coming up?"

"In a minute," Jake said. "I'm going to take a look at your front door first."

"Why? What's wrong with it?"

"I don't know, but it seems like every time I turn my back it's open again."

"Okay, but be careful you don't let Archie out," she said. "I don't think Todd would forgive me if he ran away again."

Emma trudged back up to the inn, pondering Jake's comment about knowing love when he saw it. In a somewhat simpler way, it was the same thing Viv had told her about seeing sparks when Todd looked at her.

She remembered how comforted she'd felt when he came to the cottage, how patiently he'd listened while she told him what was wrong. Were her friends just telling her what they thought she wanted to hear? Or was it possible that there was still something between the two of them after all these years?

As she headed for the front door, a flash of red caught her eye. A brand new Ferrari was sitting in the parking lot, its engine still cooling from the drive in. It was a beautiful car, but she didn't recognize it as one of the ghost hunters'. She went inside to see who it belonged to.

It didn't take long to find out. As Emma stepped into the lobby, she saw Clifton standing at the front desk grinning like a schoolboy. Not surprising, really. Her assistant manager was way too impressed by money and the people who flaunted it. She only hoped the Ferrari didn't belong to another nouveau riche millionaire, come to ask if she wanted to sell her property.

"Looks like we have a new arrival," she said.

"We do," said Clifton. "She just checked in."

"I thought we were full."

"We are. She's joining another one of our guests."

Whatever secret Clifton was holding on to must be good, Emma thought. Was it a movie star, perhaps? The man looked as if he might burst.

"So, tell me. Who is she?"

Clifton glanced down at the guest registry.

"Miss Gwendolyn Ashworth."

Emma shrugged. The name didn't ring a bell.

"Is she supposed to be famous or something?"

"She says she's Mr. Dwyer's fiancée," Clifton said, his eyes bright. "Apparently, he's got himself a sugar mama."

CHAPTER 17

Repairing the fence had been just the antidote Todd needed to get rid of his bad mood. When he'd left Emma's cottage, he'd been so angry he didn't dare say another word lest it be something he'd regret. Lucky for him, though, Jake wasn't the talkative type, and after an hour of hauling lumber and pulling nails from old pickets, Todd had cooled off enough to gain some perspective. It wasn't Emma he was mad at, he realized; it was himself. He just had to find a way to channel that anger into finding a solution to his problem.

Todd stepped into the shower and let the hot water course down over his head and shoulders. He'd be sore tomorrow, but for the moment he was grateful for the chance to work off his pique without hurting Emma's feelings. The fact was, she had every right to be angry with him. If someone had barged in and tried to tell him how to run his business, he'd have thrown them out, regardless of whether their advice was good or not. As soon as he was washed and dressed, he would go find her and apologize.

It wasn't the need to make amends that had preoccupied him while he and Jake rebuilt the fence, though. He knew his relationship with Gwen was on the wrong track, so why on earth was he going forward with the engagement?

When the two of them were first dating, Todd had been so blown away by the thought of being with her that he'd written off Gwen's shortcomings—her selfishness, her immaturity, even her criticism of him and his friends—as minor annoyances. At the time, Todd and his partners had been negotiating the sale of their company, and the little time he and Gwen had together seemed too precious to waste on petty arguments. Then, after she moved in with him, it was just easier to throw money at the problem than deal with it directly. Letting her redecorate the house had been good for almost six whole months of peace.

But now that the business was sold, the minor annoyances had become major headaches. Refusing to let Todd borrow "her" car—which was technically his—was bad enough, but even minor disagreements over who owned what could cause a row that lasted for days, and just as their argument over Archie had, the only way anything ever got resolved was for Todd to back down. He couldn't afford to bury his head in the sand any longer. Unless Todd wanted to live the rest of his life on Gwen's terms, things would have to change.

He stepped out of the shower and started drying himself off. Once again, Todd thought, he would be wearing the same clothes he'd had on since arriving at the Spirit Inn. Thank goodness Emma had found him some work clothes in the Lost and Found. He wrapped the towel around his waist and opened the bathroom door.

The bedroom was dark. For a moment, Todd wondered if the inn had lost power, but the bathroom fan was still running. As he reached for the switch, he saw movement on the bed and realized that someone was in the room. He grabbed the towel at his waist more firmly and took a step back.

"I think you have the wrong room."

Todd heard a giggle and the bedside lamp came on. Gwen was stretched out on the bed in her nightdress. She crooked her finger, motioning for him to come closer.

"Hey there, lover boy."

Todd was too stunned to speak. What on earth was she doing there?

His hesitation in the face of Gwen's come-on was clearly unexpected. She sat up and reached for the robe that was draped over the end of the bed. Even in the low light, Todd could see that she was pouting. Twenty-four hours ago, it might have prompted an apology. Now it just made him feel cross. He reached over and switched on the light.

"What are you doing here?" he said. "And how did you get in my room?"

"I came to see you. The nice man at the desk gave me a key."

Clifton. Even when Todd was a kid, the guy was always making trouble for him.

Gwen crossed her arms and thrust out her lower lip, making herself look even more like a petulant child. Had she always acted like this? Todd wondered. How could he have been so blind?

"I borrowed Daddy's car and left the island on the first ferry this morning to get here," she said. "If you ask me, this is a pretty lousy way to treat your fiancée."

My fiancée?

Todd felt a chill. She must have found the ring. But how?

The suitcases! After he put the ring into the zippered pouch, he'd left the room to get his clothes. When he returned, his suitcase had been moved a few inches, but he just figured Gwen had disturbed it when she took down her own. The combination was written inside the lid and he'd already entered it on his iPhone; it never occurred to him to double-check it before closing the case. Besides, the two of them were nearly identical. Why would Gwen insist upon taking one suitcase rather than the other?

Because, he thought, one was "his" and one was "hers," and if there was anything he knew about Gwendolyn Ashworth, it was that she never shared her things, not even with Todd.

What was he going to do?

"I'm sorry," he said. "You just surprised me, that's all."

"Serves you right," she said. "After the surprise you gave me."

She stuck out her left hand and fluttered her fingers; the engagement ring shone like a spotlight.

"And it's a perfect fit, too."

Todd felt his stomach sink. He'd just congratulated himself for not popping the question this weekend, and meanwhile, Gwen had been doing it for him.

"Don't feel you have to give me an answer right away," he said. "I want both of us to be sure it's right before we decide."

"Don't be silly," she said, admiring the ring. "This is exactly what I've been waiting for."

"Oh. Well, that's good."

How was he going to explain this to Emma?

Gwen looked around the room, apparently realizing that her girl-on-the-bed routine hadn't yielded the results she'd been hoping for. She slipped her arms into the robe and wrapped it around herself, cinching the belt with a petulant tug. In his present state of mind, Todd found her performance more irritating than amusing. He grabbed his clothes and retreated to the bathroom.

"I'll be out in a minute," he said.

Todd shut the door and stared in the mirror at his own pale

face. How was he going to tell Gwen that he hadn't meant for her to find the ring? His comment that she should take her time deciding whether or not to marry him had been quickly brushed away; it wouldn't be easy to bring up the subject again. If she thought he was calling off the engagement, there was no telling what she might do. Gwen's temper was legendary.

And what about Emma? Had she been there when Clifton gave Gwen the key? He doubted it. Handing a registered guest's key to a stranger was highly unusual, if not downright illegal; Emma would never have allowed it. And yet, in spite of the risks, that was exactly what Clifton had done. Todd had a sinking feeling that the old guy had known exactly what he was doing.

As he got dressed, Todd tried to figure out how he could talk to Emma. He wished he'd taken the time to apologize to her before going back to his hotel room. It would have been a lot easier to explain the situation with Gwen if he knew she wasn't still angry with him for being a jerk. The last thing he wanted was for her to think that any of this was his idea.

When Todd stepped back into the bedroom, he found Gwen fully dressed, sitting on the chair beside the bed.

"I'm hungry," she said. "How about dinner?"

Todd hesitated. Now that they both knew she had the ring, he'd been hoping Gwen would go back to the island, but maybe this would work, too. While she got ready to go out, he could go find Emma and explain what had happened.

"Sounds good," he said. "There's a lecture I was thinking of going to later. If you'd like, maybe you can come with me."

It was only fair, he told himself. Once the lecture was over, he'd decide what to do next.

She slid out of the chair and headed for the bathroom.

"I'm going to freshen up a bit. Daddy's car was a monster

to drive up here. Why don't you go put our names in at the restaurant and I'll meet you there in a few?"

"Good idea."

This was perfect, he thought. He'd drop by Emma's office on the way, tell her what was going on, and fill her in on the details later. He opened the door.

"Um, you're not seriously thinking of going like that, are you?"

Todd glanced down at his clothes. Gwen was right. The restaurant was a pretty swanky place—too nice for a T-shirt and jeans.

"I would, but I can't open my suitcase," he said. "I forgot to write down the combination."

Gwen rolled her eyes.

"Hang on," she said, taking out her phone. "I've got it."

When Todd had changed, he looked at himself in the mirror. The shirt was a bit wrinkled, but his sweater hid most of it and the slacks didn't look too bad. Gwen straightened his collar and nodded her approval. He grabbed his keys and put them in his pocket.

"By the way," she said, "what's the lecture about?"

"Ghosts."

"Ghosts?" Gwen blanched. "As in dead people?"

"Yeah." Todd opened the door and smiled. "Didn't you know? This place is haunted."

CHAPTER 18

Emma walked into her office and shut the door feeling angrier and more hurt than she'd thought possible. Angry at Clifton for giving a guest's key to a stranger just to prove he was right about Todd, and hurt because Todd had let her believe she still meant something to him. She collapsed in her chair and stared at the desk, as heedless of her surroundings as a blind man.

She had been blind, Emma told herself. Blinded by her loneliness, blinded by longing and desire and a foolish belief that she knew anything about Todd Dwyer. Why had he come there in the first place? Was seeing her again just a way for Todd to tie up loose ends before he settled down? Archie's running away when he did had certainly been convenient. What better way to convince Emma to let down her guard than for her old sweetheart to show up looking for his little lost dog? She closed her eyes and a tear crept down her cheek.

What a fool I am.

It was Clifton's comment that Gwendolyn Ashworth was Todd's "sugar mama" that hurt the most. The idea that he might be a kept man simply didn't fit with the Todd Dwyer she'd thought she knew. In spite of her disappointment, Emma refused to believe that the boy she once loved had changed so completely. Emma decided to do some detective work. She turned to her computer and typed in the name "Gwendolyn Ashworth." If the woman in Todd's room was who and what Clifton claimed, then Google would tell her.

But as the search results came up, Emma's heart sank. Gwendolyn Ashworth was not only rich; she and her wealthy parents, Tyler and "Tippi" Ashworth, were well known in Seattle's social circles. Emma clicked on a link to the Flash + Talk section of *Seattle* magazine and found an article about a charity dinner supporting the local art museum, accompanied by a full-color photo of Gwendolyn Ashworth. Smiling for the camera, draped in jewels, she was clutching the arm of a tuxedo-clad man who looked very much like Todd.

No, Emma corrected herself, a man who *was* Todd. She felt sick.

Clifton was right. As unlikely as it seemed, Todd had caught the fancy of a rich girl and used that connection to work his way into the city's social scene. She felt bile rise in her throat and swallowed hard as she studied the man in the photo. Even as the proof of his dishonesty was staring her in the face, she refused to believe it.

Emma scrolled down the page, looking for the caption. The letters on the screen swam as she saw Todd's name. Seeing it in black and white felt like a stab wound to her heart. But it was the rest of the caption that left her reeling, so stunned she had to grab the desk to keep from falling out of her chair.

"*Gwendolyn Ashworth arrives at the reception,*" the caption read, "*accompanied by Mr. Todd Dwyer, Silicon Forest's newest multi-millionaire.*"

Emma didn't know how long she'd been staring at the screen when she heard the knock at her door. She quickly shut down her computer and wiped her hands down her face, hoping to rid it of any traces of the shock she'd just been given.

"Come in."

The door opened and her housekeeper, Lupita, poked her head inside.

"Sorry to bother you," she said. "I need the key to the cottage."

"Oh! Sorry, Lupe. I forgot it was wash day."

Having the housekeepers take care of her dirty linens was one of the perks of being the inn's manager, but it necessitated their having a key and Jake had just changed the lock on her front door. Emma fished the shiny new key out of her top drawer.

"I didn't strip the bed yet."

"That's all right," Lupita said. "I'll take care of it."

When the door closed, Emma went back to her computer and did another search. Not for Gwendolyn Ashworth this time, but for Todd Dwyer. The results were staggering.

According to Wikipedia, Todd wasn't just rich; he was some kind of computer genius. He'd also written a game app for smart phones called Pop Up Pups, which was making millions more for a man who "eschewed publicity" and "guarded his privacy like a monk."

Emma clicked back to the picture of Todd and Gwendolyn. He didn't look like any monk she'd ever heard of.

She turned off the computer and sat back, thinking about everything he'd told her in light of this new information. When Todd had said he was "between jobs" and "working part-time at home" she assumed he was unemployed, or nearly so. He hadn't been lying, exactly, but he'd certainly been evasive. And what about not having any clothes to wear and driving a broken-down old Jeep? If the folks at Wikipedia were right, Todd should have been wearing *GQ* duds and driving a fancy car. Maybe that Ferrari in the parking lot was actually his. Once again, Emma found herself wondering what it was that had brought Todd to the inn.

There was another knock on the door. Lupita, she thought, returning Emma's key.

"Come in, Lupe," she said. "Thank you for—"

It was Todd. Showered and changed, wearing a cashmere sweater and wool slacks, he looked less like a construction worker and more like the successful Internet entrepreneur that he was.

Dear God, did I really tell him I knew more about business than he did?

He stepped into the room and closed the door.

"I'd say you're welcome, but I'm not sure what I'm being thanked for."

"Please leave," she said, feeling her face grow hot.

"In a minute," Todd told her. "I have something to tell you first."

"I already know about your fiancée, if that's what you're going to tell me."

The look on Todd's face was so pained that for an instant, Emma almost felt sorry for him.

Don't let him fool you. It's only an act.

"I'll get to that in a moment," he said. "First, I owe you an apology. I shouldn't have tried to tell you how to run your business this morning. I'm sorry."

"Yeah, well, I guess it just proves what an idiot I am," she said. "I don't even know good advice when I hear it."

Todd shook his head. "Whether it was good advice or not, it wasn't what you needed. You poured your heart out to a friend and got treated like a business student. I should have told you at the time that I was wrong, but I was upset. I needed some time to cool off."

In spite of herself, Emma could feel her resistance weakening. Todd seemed sincere, and the fact was, he hadn't told her anything back at the cottage that she didn't already know. If Gwendolyn hadn't shown up when she did, Emma might have been apologizing to him.

But Gwendolyn had shown up, and Todd's apology was nothing more than a feint to keep Emma from discovering the real reason he'd come to the Spirit Inn.

Of course, she thought, her anger reviving. Why hadn't she thought of it before?

"The thing about Gwen is, she's not really my fiancée," Todd said. "I'd been planning to propose to her this weekend, but I changed my mind."

Emma smirked. "And you let her keep the ring? Wow, that's some consolation prize."

He looked at her fiercely. "This isn't easy for me. I came here as a friend to try to explain what's been going on."

She stood and leaned across her desk.

"No, you've been lying to me since you got here, and now that I've got an inkling of what's really going on, you're trying to throw me off the scent."

"What are you talking about?"

"Oh, come on. I may be slow, but I'm not stupid."

Emma smirked again. Now that she understood what was happening, it was almost funny to see how easily she'd been fooled.

"You came up to the inn and checked out the property under the guise of looking for your lost dog. Then you stayed the night so you could survey the inn, all the while doing your best to discover what my financial position is."

Todd looked stunned.

"I wasn't checking anything out; I was looking for Archie."

"So you say."

"I do say! Furthermore, I didn't ask to stay the night; *you* offered me a room."

"For *free*," she said, laughing at her own naïveté. "I should have made you pay for it."

"I was going to." He looked away and said more softly, "I'm still going to."

"Don't bother," Emma snapped. "And tell Miss Ashworth not to get her heart set on this place, either. There are plenty of other banks out there. I'm not selling out to you or anybody else."

"What?"

"Oh, please. Don't act like you don't know what I'm talking about. The only reason you came in here was to try to keep me from figuring out why Gwendolyn showed up all of a sudden. How long after you knew about my loan did it take you to call and tell her to come take a look at this place? You wouldn't be the first rich guy to make me an offer for it, you know. I'll bet you figured I'd let you have it for cheap, too, us being old friends and all."

Todd's face darkened. When he spoke again, his lips were tight.

"You're insane if you think I came here with an eye to buying this place. I told you the first night I got here, and it's the truth: Archie ran away and led me here. As far as Gwen goes, our so-called engagement is a misunderstanding. I have no intention of marrying her.

"What's really disappointing, though, is that you seem angry with me for being successful," he continued. "You're not the only one who had it tough as a kid, you know. Yes, I've been lucky, but I've worked hard, too, and I gave up a lot to get where I am."

"Like what?" she said. "You've got your fancy girlfriend and your sports car and more money than most people ever dream of. Name one thing you've given up to get where you are. Just *one.*"

Todd swallowed and looked at her steadily.

"You," he said. "I gave you up, and I'm sorry."

For just a moment, Emma could picture Todd—a fatherless boy with the care of his whole family resting on his shoulders—and her heart went out to him. Maybe he hadn't had a choice, she thought. Maybe he did regret cutting her off the way he did.

Then Emma remembered how she'd waited at the post office, day after day, hoping to hear from the boy who'd sworn he loved her and promised to write. It wasn't just a summertime crush. Emma had seen Todd's love as proof that she was more than an addict's kid or a burden for her grandmother to bear; she was someone special, someone worth thinking about even when she was miles away. It would have been easier if Todd had just said he didn't care, Emma thought. Not writing had meant she wasn't even worth the price of a stamp.

"Maybe so," she said. "But you can't have me back just because it's convenient."

CHAPTER 19

Gwen was outside the restaurant when Todd returned, standing with a group of people who were listening to a man Todd had seen several times since his arrival. He was tall and angular, with a shock of white hair, a beak of a nose, and a birdlike strut, and his presence at the inn was as ubiquitous as the Van Vandevanders'.

As Todd joined the group, Gwen gave him a buss on the cheek and the man ceased pontificating long enough for her to introduce him to the others. Todd smiled amiably and accepted a glass of champagne from a passing waiter. After his tardy arrival, he'd been expecting a chillier reception.

"Dr. Richards has just been telling us about his theory," Gwen said, indicating the white-haired man.

Todd took a sip of his drink. "About what?"

"The origin of the unexplained phenomena here at the inn," Richards said.

"He's been working on it for *ages.*" Gwen's look was avid. "It's very interesting."

For Todd, whose years of visits to the Spirit Inn had yielded nothing in the way of supernatural encounters, the idea that the inn might be haunted was ludicrous. He found it impossible not to roll his eyes.

"I see you're here with a skeptic, Gwen."

"What's wrong with being a skeptic?" Todd said.

"Nothing." The man gave him a simpering smile. "But there's a difference between skepticism and willful denial."

"Dr. Richards is an expert on psychic phenomena," Gwen said. "He's a *scientist*."

He should probably just back down and let Richards have his fun, Todd thought, but he couldn't. Not just because he knew there was no scientific basis for any "theory" the man might have, but also because the whole idea of the inn's being haunted was destroying Emma's business and maybe even her future. As long as people still believed that the inn was haunted, it would never be the place she dreamed it could be.

"All right," he said. "Convince me. Tell me what your theory is."

"I'd be happy to." Richards looked around. "If the others here will bear with me."

When there were no objections, Todd smiled grimly.

"I'm all ears."

Dr. Richards's chest swelled with self-importance. The man was clearly in his element.

"This hotel was built by two men—business partners—who originally planned to provide lodging for the miners who passed through on their way home from the gold fields. Not as fanciful as striking a vein of ore, but a good living for an honest man.

"The first partner was happy with their arrangement, but the second was impatient to make his fortune and began robbing the lodgers as they slept, replacing the gold in their saddlebags with worthless pyrite. When the first partner discovered this, he confronted his partner and the two men fought, leaving the honest man badly wounded.

"As it happened, the hotel had been so busy that additional rooms were being added to the original structure. The greedy partner dragged the honest partner, still alive, into an unfinished portion of the hotel and completed the walls around him, leaving him to his fate."

Gwen shuddered. "That's awful."

"Immurement, as it's called, effectively buries a victim alive. Various cultures have used it for centuries as punishment, and it survives in some of the more primitive corners of the globe even today. If I'm right, immurement explains many of the world's ghost sightings, its victims still tied in death to the places where they were trapped in life."

As the others murmured to one another, Todd shook his head. Trapped inside a wall? Was this guy kidding?

Another member of the group piped up.

"I've heard of that. It's like 'The Cask of Amantillado.' "

Richards nodded. "Poe's story about a man being trapped alive behind a brick wall was probably based upon stories he'd heard about immurements in English castles. Thornton Abbey in Lincolnshire, perhaps."

"So what happened to the other partner?" the man asked.

Gwen nodded. "Did they ever find the man in the wall?"

"Well," Richards said, "that's where it gets interesting. As to the first, he fled and was killed by a miner who, having discovered he'd been robbed and guessing who the perpetrator was, had been on his way back to settle the score. However, when the cheated man searched his victim's possessions, he found that the dishonest man, too, had only pyrite in his saddlebags."

"So what happened to the gold?"

"No one knows. Some believe he'd hidden it elsewhere; some say he'd spent it all."

Gwen was rapt. "And what do you think?"

The good doctor smiled.

"I believe that the honest partner, upon discovering what the other had done, decided to teach his partner a lesson by replacing the gold he'd stolen with pyrite, just as that man's victims' gold had been."

"So he was a thief, too."

"Or perhaps he intended to give the gold back to its rightful owners. It remains a mystery."

"You mean they didn't find the gold with his body?"

"I'm afraid that neither gold nor body was ever found. The hotel fell into disrepair and was sold to satisfy tax liens. The owners couldn't keep a work crew on-site long enough to effect the needed repairs and it remained unoccupied for years. My understanding is that it was only fully restored about twenty years ago."

In spite of himself, Todd had been briefly caught up in the man's story, but his mention of when the inn was restored brought him back to reality. According to Richards, the restoration had been completed about the same time that Todd and his family had started coming there. Interesting, he thought, that no one had ever mentioned the place being haunted back then.

"You mean no one's ever looked for the partner or the gold?" Gwen asked.

Richards shook his head.

"Some feared that to do so might invite the wrath of the dead man's spirit."

Todd pursed his lips. There were no ghosts; there'd been no treasure; none of what he'd heard was real. It was just a tale that someone had made up for their own purposes. Did Emma know that? Or had she been taken in just like the ghost hunters?

"That's an interesting story," he said, "but you have to admit it's pretty far-fetched. Without any evidence to back it up, I'm afraid I remain a skeptic."

"I thought you might," Richards said. "Nevertheless, many of us here are inclined to believe it."

"And why is that?"

"Because," the man said, rapping a knuckle against the ornate wallpaper, "some of these walls are hollow."

"I don't know why you had to be so rude to Dr. Richards," Gwen hissed as the two of them looked over their menus. "I thought his story was very interesting."

"I wasn't being rude," Todd said. "I'm just not as gullible as the rest of the Kool-Aid drinkers around here."

Her lips tightened. "I suppose you're including me in that group."

Todd paused a moment to collect his thoughts. In the last forty-eight hours, he'd had to deal with a series of surprising and emotionally wrenching incidents, most of which had been precipitated by Gwen. He was finding it hard not to lose his temper.

"I'm sorry," he said. "I didn't mean to be insulting, but my family stayed here lots of times when I was a kid and my parents knew the owner pretty well. She never said anything about the place being haunted."

"You never told me that. Sort of a strange coincidence, you just happening to show up here."

He frowned. "I didn't just 'show up' here. Archie ran away and I followed him."

"Hmm," she said, returning her attention to the menu. "So you knew the manager back then?"

Todd was looking over the wine list. He hadn't made up

his mind about the entrée, but he'd need some alcohol if he was going to get through this meal.

"Yes," he said. "She was very nice. Her granddaughter owns the place now."

"Was that your little girlfriend?"

He looked up. "Who told you about her?"

"Your mother."

Todd felt his lips tighten. *So Ma did tell her about Emma.*

"Oh, don't worry," Gwen said, seeing the look on his face. "This was months ago, back when you and I first got serious. Your mother told me she was glad you'd finally fallen in love again. Apparently, she'd been feeling guilty all these years for keeping the two of you apart."

She gave him a simpering smile.

"So when I got your message, I thought maybe I should get up here and make sure you weren't having any second thoughts."

Todd sat back. No wonder Gwen had hightailed it up there in her father's Ferrari. Having finally gotten the ring she wanted, she'd been anxious to protect her investment.

"I'm not sure I would have called Emma my girlfriend," he said. "She and Claire and I had some good times here as kids. She's been keeping Archie for me while I'm here."

"Well, when you see her again, maybe you could introduce us."

When the waiter had taken their orders, Gwen looked around.

"This is a nice place."

"It is," Todd said, glad to be changing the subject. "I'm glad I changed my clothes, too."

"Did you notice who the chef de cuisine is?"

"No. Does it matter?"

Gwen gave him a disdainful look.

"Of course it *matters,* especially considering the man is a felon. He used to be a celebrity until he got caught dealing drugs out of his flagship restaurant. It was a huge scandal. Honestly, I can't believe he's out of jail already."

Todd shook his head. "Must not be the same guy."

"Of course it is," she said. "There was a picture of him in the back of the menu. I never forget a face."

He vaguely recalled seeing the picture of Jean-Paul when he was flipping through the menu, but the name hadn't rung a bell. Besides, what difference did it make? If it had been that much of a scandal, Emma would already know about it. Then again, a drug habit could be very expensive.

Todd was just wondering whether her chef's situation had anything to do with Emma's financial difficulties when the calm of the restaurant was shattered by an ear-piercing scream.

CHAPTER 20

Emma bolted out of her office and looked around.

"Who was that? What happened?"

Clifton was behind the desk, looking stunned.

"I'm not sure," he said. "It seems to have come from the utility room."

She stepped around the counter and saw Lupita running down the hall toward her, wide-eyed and babbling hysterically. Guests in the lobby scattered as the heavyset woman charged into their midst and collapsed in Emma's arms.

"Una fantasma," Lupita sobbed. *"En la lavandería. Lo vi. Lo vi."*

A ghost in the laundry room?

Emma glared at her front-desk staff. This was what happened when rumors got out of control. Lupita was the most levelheaded employee she had. If she was seeing ghosts, it wouldn't be long before the entire inn descended into chaos.

She helped the older woman to a chair and looked around.

"Adam, get Lupita a glass of water and stay with her until I get back. I'm going to go check out the laundry room."

Emma patted the housekeeper's broad back.

"Stay here, Lupe. I'll be back in a minute."

Frightened faces peered out from the guest rooms as

Emma headed down the hall. When this was over, she'd have to go door-to-door and assure them that they were in no danger.

Unfortunately, Emma had not been the only person who'd heard Lupita's claim about a ghost, and as she turned the corner, she saw half a dozen people standing in the hall outside the laundry room, talking excitedly amid the noise from the open door. As Emma approached, she was dismayed to see that one of them was Gwendolyn Ashworth.

"Excuse me," she said, pushing past.

The roar inside was daunting. Towels sloshed noisily in the washers and clean sheets tumbled in a row of miniature tornados, creating a turbulence that could be felt as well as heard. The floor was strewn with dirty linens that Emma instantly recognized as those that had been gathered from her cottage. Lupita must have just emptied them onto the floor, she thought, when the "ghost" appeared.

Dr. Richards loomed over the pile like a detective at a crime scene. Todd, squatting in front of him, was examining a small white blanket.

"*Is that blood?*" Richards said, struggling to make himself heard above the din.

"It's pizza sauce." Emma stepped forward and snatched the blanket out of Todd's hands. "What are you doing in here?"

"Looking for clues," Richards said, indicating the pile in front of them. "Under the circumstances, we thought it best to get down here quickly."

Emma glanced at Todd and his gaze slipped sideways. He didn't believe in ghosts, she thought. What was this all about?

At least he has the decency to look ashamed.

She motioned for the two of them to follow her out of the room.

"I really wish you'd talked to me first before charging down here and scaring the daylights out of my guests."

Richards looked around at the others.

"I'd hardly call this a stampede," he sniffed.

She ignored him.

"Holding your convention here doesn't give you the right to snoop into every corner of the inn. There are guests here who have nothing to do with ghost hunting and they have a right to enjoy their stay without being disturbed by your so-called investigation. I've already given permission for a séance tonight, but until then, I'd prefer that you confine your inquiries to the areas we've set aside for your use."

Richards tossed his head, sending the shock of white hair flying.

"As you wish. I suppose there's no reason for us to remain here anyway."

He glanced around at the others.

"Even a rapid response can't guarantee a positive result, I'm afraid. Come along."

Todd hesitated a moment, then shook his head and followed the others.

When everyone had left, Emma spent a few minutes going through the pile on the floor. There was nothing there that could even remotely have been mistaken for a ghost. Whatever frightened Lupita had existed only in her imagination.

The lobby was considerably quieter when Emma returned. Lupita was still in her chair, the glass of water clutched in her hand. Adam stood by, guarding her from Dr. Richards and his group, who hovered nearby, talking among themselves and darting hopeful glances at the housekeeper.

Quieter, however, did not mean calmer. Lupita's screams might have died down, but their effect was still very much in evidence. Looking around the lobby, Emma noted the tense, troubled looks on the faces of her guests and the forced, high-pitched laughter that substituted for genuine amusement. Even

Clifton, who had remained at his post behind the front desk, appeared shaken.

"Don't tell me you've seen a ghost, too," she whispered.

He shook his head. "No, but I think I may have heard one."

"Oh, for pity's sake."

Was everyone but her losing their mind?

Adam caught her eye and nodded.

"I heard it, too," he said softly.

Oh, great. This is all I need.

"Come on, you guys," she said. "Don't start freaking out on me."

The two of them exchanged a look and nodded their agreement, but it was clear they weren't convinced. Emma was about to explain the concept of a self-fulfilling prophecy when she heard a harsh scratching sound. It seemed to be coming from no place in particular and everywhere at once. Dr. Richards hurried over, a look of eager anticipation on his face.

"I believe we may have encountered another anomaly."

Before Emma could stop him, Adam piped up.

"It started right after Lupe saw the ghost!"

People were beginning to crowd around them. Some looked apprehensive, but many seemed excited at the prospect of a supernatural encounter.

"Don't panic," Emma said. "It's probably just a raccoon in the crawl space."

There was a loud thump overhead, followed by a low rumble that was almost a growl. Everyone stared at the ceiling. Lupita crossed herself and Adam paled. Emma gave the two of them a determined smile, hoping they would take the hint. So what if they'd heard a strange noise? The inn was *supposed* to be haunted, right?

She heard footsteps approaching and saw Lars Van Vandevander bustle into the room with Viv and the steering committee trailing behind like ducklings. Smiling broadly, he began canvassing the room, gathering details from the SSSPA members who'd witnessed the encounter and congratulating them on their good fortune.

Viv detached herself from the group and wandered through the lobby, the bells on her shoes jingling softly as she touched the walls and furniture. Every few steps, she stopped and closed her eyes as if listening for something, then opened them and continued on. When she'd covered the entire room, she walked back to her husband and whispered something in his ear.

What was that all about? Emma wondered.

Dr. Richards joined them and the Van Vandevanders spoke quietly to him for a few seconds more before consulting the other committee members, who nodded in agreement. The professor straightened up and clapped his hands.

"May I have your attention, please?" he said, addressing the room. "What you have just witnessed is further evidence of the paranormal outpouring which commenced here last night. Fortunately, we have among us a highly sensitive medium in my wife, Vivienne. Based upon her vibrational readings, we believe it is crucial that we open a dialogue with these manifestations as quickly as possible. A confluence like this is quite literally a once-in-a-lifetime occurrence. I'm sure that none of us wants to see it wasted."

Emma shook her head. What was he thinking? They couldn't hold the séance now. The Energy Room had already been set up for Lars's lecture; it would take time to restage it for the séance. She hurried over and pulled him aside.

"I thought we agreed to wait until after your lecture, Professor."

"Impossible," he said. "There's no time to lose."

"But the Energy Room isn't set up for a séance."

"We won't be using the Energy Room," he said. "We'll be using the Spirit Room as we originally planned."

Lars's face had taken on a stubborn cast, and the rest of the committee members looked as implacable as he did. Emma glanced back at the front desk, hoping her assistant manager might back her up in the face of their opposition, but Clifton was no longer there.

"All right," she said, feeling defeated. "I'll send someone down to help you set up the room."

"Wonderful!" Lars said. "You won't be sorry, believe me. This will be a night to remember."

CHAPTER 21

Todd and Gwendolyn had finished their dinner in relative silence. Gwen tried to make a brief pitch for a friend of her father's who wanted to help Todd "take his apps to the next level," but when it became clear that he had no interest in pursuing it, she confined herself to polishing off the eighty-dollar bottle of Shiraz. Todd, meanwhile, sat glumly pushing food around his plate as the tables around them emptied. Since the incident in the laundry room, every scratch, bump, or other odd sound at the inn had been attributed to ghostly presences, and the general consensus was that it was better to be with the experts at the séance than to take one's chances alone in a hotel room.

Todd's mood had sunk from merely sad to despairing. Gwen was too drunk to drive, and when he'd inquired at the front desk, they told him there were no other rooms available. For the time being, at least, he was stuck with her. He paid the check and set his napkin on the table.

"Why don't we skip the séance?" he said. "I'd rather turn in early."

"But I want to go," Gwen whined. "Why do you have to be so mean?"

"I'm not being mean. I'm just tired."

"What is with you? We get engaged and the next thing I know you've turned into this massive buzzkill. Why did you even give me a ring if you were going to be like this?"

"I didn't give you that ring," he muttered. "If our suitcases hadn't been switched, you'd never have known about it."

Gwen drew her left hand to her chest and clutched it like a miser with a gold coin.

"That's not true! You left it in there for me to find."

Todd knew he should leave it at that, but having finally said something true and honest to her, he found he couldn't stop.

"And another thing," he said. "I'm not interested in driving myself into an early grave like my father did, so please stop badgering me to start another company. I've made it; I'm doing well; I need a rest."

Gwen's eyes narrowed.

"This is her fault, isn't it? You think if you hook up with her again, you'll be able to recapture your 'lost youth' or whatever."

Todd had to think about that. Was seeing Emma again what had caused his change of heart? Coming back to the Spirit Inn had certainly reminded him that a simpler, more balanced life was possible, but that had been a dream of his for years, something that until recently he'd been sure that Gwen wanted, too. But if it wasn't Emma's doing, then what was it?

He smiled as the truth dawned on him.

Archie.

Archie, whose carefree life with Uncle Bertie had been the opposite of the oppressive grind Todd had been putting himself through and which Gwen expected him to continue indefinitely; a happy little mutt who wanted nothing more than to make people laugh and smile and cheer him on; the sweet and loving animal that Gwen had ordered Todd to get rid of.

Archie had led him back to the one place where Todd could see who he might have become if he hadn't lost his father when he did. Maybe it was just a coincidence, but it was still pretty remarkable.

Gwen's look was contrite. She reached across the table and touched his hand.

"I'm sorry," she said. "I should have realized you weren't ready to start another company. You know how Daddy is, always a million deals going in his head. And as far as the ring goes, maybe I should have asked you about it first. It's just that when I saw it, I mean, it was the one we'd seen at the jeweler's and I—"

He shook his head. "No, no. Of course you'd just assume . . ."

Todd felt like a heel. He'd been making the assumption that Gwen wouldn't be interested in a simpler life, but had he ever really asked?

"Losing Uncle Bertie was really hard for you," she said. "And then with Archie running away like he did, I'm sure you were super stressed-out."

"You're right." He nodded. "Thanks for understanding."

"So, come on," she said. "Let's go to the séance. We can sleep in late and still have plenty of time to get the little pooch to Claire's house."

Todd just stared at her. Nothing had changed, he realized. Gwen was still pushing her own agenda with no thought as to what he wanted. He pulled his hand away.

"No. You can go by yourself if you'd like, but I'm not going."

"Why not?" she snapped, her face reddening.

"Because," he said, "I'd just feel silly sitting there, pretending that something spooky is going on. There are no such things as ghosts."

"The maid saw a ghost in the laundry room and something was scratching inside the walls. How else do you explain *that?*"

Todd had been pondering that himself.

"A tree branch rubbing against the siding or a raccoon in the crawl space could make that kind of noise. You don't need a ghost to explain it."

"What about the laundry room? The maid said a ghost appeared right in front of her."

Gwen was halfway out of her chair, her voice barely softer than a shout. Todd struggled to remain calm.

"She'd just dumped everything out on the floor," he said. "There could have been a pocket of air inside; maybe a draft blew the blanket and she thought it moved."

"Or maybe it was the spirit of the man in the walls," Gwen said. "Just like Dr. Richards told us."

"Okay," he said. "What if that were true? Richards claims the ghost is tied to the inn, but Emma said the housekeeper had just brought those things in from her place. If there was a ghost in those things, it had to have come from there. And believe me, there's no ghost living in Emma's cottage."

The answer struck Todd with the force of a hammer blow. Lars and Viv had told him the first encounter was on the same night that Archie had turned up at the cottage. Lars had described it as a low moan or keening, but a sound like that could as easily have come from a lost dog. Todd knew that Archie had been getting out of the cottage, too, and was probably responsible for at least one other encounter—the stolen sandwich he'd been eating in the bushes. If Dr. Richards was right and there were hidden passages in the inn's walls, wasn't it possible that Archie had found his way into them without being seen?

"I have to go," Todd said. "You head down to the Spirit Room and I'll meet you there in a few minutes."

He stood and headed for the exit.

"Wait a minute," Gwen yelled after him. "I thought you said you were too tired to go to the séance."

A thin layer of ice crunched under his feet as Todd ran down the path toward the cottage. Emma said that Jake had replaced the lock on her door just that morning, and Archie had been inside when Todd had seen him last. That meant the little dog was still there when the housekeeper went in to fetch the laundry. Had Archie somehow gotten out without the housekeeper seeing him? Todd dearly hoped not. If he had—and if the ghost hunters discovered it was a dog they'd been chasing, not a ghost—Emma could be in a lot of trouble.

As he drew closer, Todd found himself praying that Archie would be inside. Even though it meant that it would be harder to come up with a simple, rational reason for the encounters the ghost hunters had been experiencing that weekend, it would still be preferable to confirming that the little dog was to blame.

The Van Vandevanders, at least, knew that Todd and Emma were old friends. How much of a leap would it be for them to conclude that the two of them had decided to turn Archie loose on the property, hoping that a trained circus animal would be capable of getting into all sorts of out-of-the-way places and making his presence known? And if they did that, the fallout for Emma might be disastrous. Like anyone else, the ghost hunters would be quick to anger if they thought they were being made fun of.

The front door was locked. Todd peered through the windows; Archie wasn't on the pillow Emma had given him or anywhere he could see.

He tapped on the pane.

"Archie? Archie, you in there?"

Todd cupped his hands around his eyes, trying to cut the glare from the porch light. He saw no movement inside the cottage, no fleeting shadow that would indicate the presence of a small dog. In a last-ditch effort, he banged on the front door and yelled Archie's name, then peered through the window again.

Satisfied at last that his dog was not inside, Todd turned and headed back up to the inn. It was time to give Emma the bad news.

CHAPTER 22

Gwen walked into the Spirit Room and took a seat in the circle before doing a quick survey of the other people in the room. She hadn't come there to contact the spirits; she couldn't care less if the place was haunted or not. She was only interested in one thing: eliminating Emma as a threat to her relationship with Todd.

She'd just discovered the engagement ring in her suitcase when she got Todd's message. At first, Gwen was amused, recalling Fran's story about the Spirit Inn and Todd's childhood sweetheart. With a ring on her finger, the thought that her fiancé might suddenly change his mind seemed ludicrous, but then the odd way in which he'd delivered it began to nag at her.

Todd was a romantic at heart; it seemed out of character for him not to make a formal marriage proposal. Was it possible he hadn't meant for her to find the ring at all? Suddenly, the thought that seeing his old girlfriend might change Todd's mind about marrying Gwen didn't seem so far-fetched.

Todd hadn't told her much about Emma, but Gwen doubted that Claire had always been with them during their summers at the inn. According to his mother, the two of them had been quite serious at the end. Even without Fran's information, it had been obvious since she'd arrived that something about Todd had changed since Gwen saw him last. The last few hours, in fact, had been downright unnerving. What had happened to the guy who always put her needs first?

The chairs around her were quickly filling up. A handsome older woman Gwen had seen in the restaurant stepped into the room and looked around for an open seat. Tall and elegant, with platinum hair that fell to her shoulders, she looked a bit like Lauren Bacall. The woman intrigued her, and when she walked over and asked if she could sit beside her, Gwen happily agreed. Why, she wondered, would someone like that be interested in ghosts?

Before she could ask, however, Emma walked into the room. Gwen watched with narrowed eyes as her rival crossed the room to speak with Professor Van Vandevander. The girl was awfully plain, she thought, and that outfit did nothing for her figure. What could Todd possibly see in her? Then again, a man's head could be turned by the strangest things. Gwen's mother was far better looking than her stepmother, yet her father had pursued Tippi like a hound after a hare. She'd be damned if she let Todd do the same thing to her.

Gwen slowly moved her left hand so that the diamonds on her engagement ring caught the light. In general, she preferred giving subtle signals to the competition, but she wasn't above doing something overt if they didn't take the hint. As Emma and the professor continued their chat, Gwen glanced toward the door, hoping Todd would join her soon.

"Hello again," a voice said.

She looked back and saw Dr. Richards approaching.

"I'm glad to see you here," he said. "I was afraid you'd decided not to come."

"Oh, no," she said smoothly. "You couldn't keep me away."

"Have you met Dee?" He indicated the woman sitting

next to her. "She's been a member of our chapter almost as long as I have."

"No." Gwen shook her head. "I'm afraid I haven't."

He leaned closer.

"Dee, this is Gwen. She and I met this evening. Her husband, Todd, is one of our skeptics."

Dee offered her a cool, dry hand. "Pleased to meet you."

"The same," Gwen said as they shook. "But Todd's not my husband. Not yet, anyway."

She fluttered the fingers of her left hand. "Don't you love it?"

"Congratulations," Richards said.

Dee nodded. "It's very nice."

Gwen saw Van Vandevander approach with Emma trailing behind.

"Have you got a moment, Dick?"

"In a minute," Richards said. "Dee and I were just congratulating Miss Ashworth on her engagement."

He pointed at Gwen's ring.

"Oh." The professor glanced nervously at Emma. "Congratulations."

"Emma, have you met Gwen?"

"Briefly," she said, giving the ring a quick glance. "Congrats."

Gwen leaned forward confidentially.

"Actually, Emma and Todd knew each other when they were kids." She winked. "I think it was puppy love."

Her comment had the desired effect. Emma's face reddened and she laughed nervously.

"Don't know where you got that idea."

"Oh? Well, maybe Todd was just trying to make me jealous," Gwen said. "Either way, I'm relieved. I wouldn't want us to be enemies."

The awkward moment left everyone at a momentary loss.

"So," Richards said. "You needed to talk to me, Lars?"

"Yes," the professor said. "In private, if you don't mind."

As the other three walked away, Gwen turned back to the woman next to her.

"So, you've been to a lot of these conventions, have you?"

Dee smiled. "A few, yes."

"I hope you don't mind my asking, but what keeps bringing you back? Have you ever actually seen a ghost at one of these things?"

As the older woman took a moment to think, Gwen noticed something she hadn't before. Dee wasn't just fashionably thin; she was gaunt, and her shoulder-length platinum tresses were almost certainly an expensive wig, rather than her real hair. The color in her cheeks was a light touch of rouge, too, and though her pale skin showed none of the ravages caused by sun exposure, it was so thin that Gwen could clearly see the web of blue veins underneath. Gwen squirmed. Sickness, death, and old age had always made her uncomfortable.

"No," Dee said at last, "I can't say I've ever seen a ghost at one of these things, but I have friends who claim they did."

"Well, you can always hope, I guess."

"Yes," Dee said. "I'm afraid that hope is all I have now."

She lifted Gwen's hand and examined the ring again.

"Your Todd must be very generous."

"He is," Gwen said. "He knows how to keep me happy."

"My husband was generous, too. Not that he could have afforded a ring like that, but he gave me more love and laughter in twenty-one years than most people get in a lifetime."

Dee had a faraway look in her eyes.

"I'm not sure I ever thanked him enough for that. I suppose that's why I come here," she said. "I keep wishing there was some way I could tell him."

Gwen slowly withdrew her hand.

"When did you . . . lose him?"

"Hmm? Oh, Archie's been gone for almost fifteen years now."

"Your husband's name was Archie?"

"Short for Archibald, yes, but he hated that." She laughed. "I'm not even sure he liked the name Archie, come to think of it, but it suited him."

Gwen almost said something about Uncle Bertie's dog, but decided not to. What were the chances? she thought. She'd have to be sure to tell Todd when he arrived. She gave Dee a thin smile and glanced at the door again. What on earth was keeping him?

Emma charged into the lobby and barked at Adam.

"Has he shown up yet?"

"No. Sorry." He shrugged apologetically. "He just said he'd be back for the séance."

"Well, it's about to start and I can't find him anywhere."

She ran a hand partway through her hair and yanked, hoping the pain would help her focus. Big things were happening; her assistant manager was AWOL; and all she could think about was Todd's stupid fiancée. If Adam hadn't been standing six feet away from her, she'd have screamed in frustration.

"All right," she said, "we'll just have to move on without him. You stay here and take care of the guests. Don't worry if you can't answer the phones; they can go to voice mail for now. If anyone starts freaking out, I don't want you to be stuck on the phone."

The desk clerk looked crestfallen.

"I guess that means I can't go to the séance, huh?"

"Adam, you know I love you, but I cannot deal with your disappointment right now. Unless by some miracle Clifton shows up this very second, the answer is no, absolutely not."

She heard footsteps and saw Todd coming toward her down the hallway.

"I need to talk to you," he said. "It's urgent."

Emma held up her hand.

"Nope. Sorry. No time to chat," she said as she headed toward her office. "She's waiting for you in the Spirit Room."

"Who, Gwen? No." He shook his head. "I need to talk to *you. Right now.*"

Emma worked her jaw, glancing from Todd to an open-mouthed Adam. Why was he doing this to her? Wasn't it bad enough that he'd told his fiancée that the two of them had been sweet on each other as kids? For a little while there, she'd thought Todd was still her friend, that maybe she'd misjudged him, but after Gwen's crack about puppy love, Emma realized that the two of them had been laughing behind her back all along.

Even so, he was a guest and she could hardly tell her staff to treat the guests well if she wasn't prepared to do the same. She forced herself to smile.

"All right. What can I help you with?"

Todd hesitated. "I'd rather talk in your office, if you don't mind."

"Of course," she said. "Adam, I'll be out in a minute. If Clifton shows up, please buzz me right away."

Todd followed her into her office and Emma closed the door behind him.

"What do you want?" she snapped. "Or did you just drop by to give me more advice about how to run my business?"

"It's Archie," Todd said. "I think he may be your ghost."

She almost laughed. Archie a ghost? Was this a joke?

"The first night I was here, remember? Lars and Viv told me they heard a ghost howling."

Emma frowned, recalling Viv's despondency when the spirits had refused to show themselves.

"No, that was the day after. There weren't any encounters the first day."

Todd shook his head. "The next morning, then. Lars said it was around midnight when they heard it. Then you told me that Archie showed up at the cottage around two, right?"

She thought about that for a moment.

"Yeah, I suppose, but I didn't hear him howl."

"I didn't say you did. Remember that thorn he had in his paw? Jake and I found one of those bushes near the toolshed. If that was where Archie stepped on it, anyone on the east side of the building would have heard him howl."

Emma thought about that. The Van Vandevanders' room was on that side. If Archie had howled when he stepped on the spiny cocklebur, they would have been in the best position to hear him. But that was silly, she told herself. They'd have realized it was a dog, surely.

"Archie stole the sandwich, too," Todd said. "I saw him with it in his mouth, but I thought the kitchen staff had given it to him. When somebody told me later that they thought a ghost had taken it, I didn't bother to tell them. It just seemed like a harmless mistake."

With the evidence piling up, Emma could feel her anxiety growing. What if Archie *was* the reason for the encounters?

"But the scratching and the other sounds, like someone walking overhead. . . ."

"I think I can explain those, too," Todd said. "Or at least some of them. Dr. Richards told us he thinks there are hidden passages behind the walls. What if Archie got in there somehow? I know it sounds crazy, but . . ."

"No," she said. "It's not crazy. He's right; there are empty spaces in the walls."

Todd's jaw dropped. "You knew about them?"

"Of course. That's why the inn is so hard to maintain. There are places we can't even get to inside. Not without breaking through the roof or the walls, anyway."

And if Archie was in there, Emma thought, how would they ever get him out?

"The ghost in the laundry room," she said, thinking aloud. "Lupita had just emptied out the linens from the cottage. Archie's blanket was in there."

"That's what I thought, too," Todd said. "Maybe he was trying to get the blanket back when Lupita grabbed the hamper. He's small and he doesn't weigh all that much. If she piled some sheets on top and picked everything up, Archie might have stayed quiet, thinking it was a game."

Archie had been playing a game with his blanket that afternoon, Emma thought. What if Todd was right and Archie thought Lupita was playing a game with him? When she dumped the laundry out on the floor, she must have seen the blanket move and thought it was alive.

If the ghost hunters find out, they'll think I set them up.

"Maybe we've got it wrong. Maybe Archie's still inside the cottage."

Todd shook his head.

"I just checked; he's not there," he said. "I'm sorry."

Emma looked around, trying to think of what she should do. Everyone was already gathered in the Spirit Room. Maybe the best thing to do was just hope for the best and go searching for Archie once the séance was over. If Todd was right, Lars and Viv had already heard Archie's cries and failed to recognize them. In the bewitching atmosphere of the séance, even a skeptical person might believe he was hearing ghosts, and there seemed little chance that Archie would bark as long as no one called his name.

"Oh, no." Emma grabbed Todd's arm. "Your dog's name is *Archie.*"

"Um, yeah," he said, smiling uncertainly. "I thought you knew that."

"Noooo," she moaned. "Why didn't I think of this before?"

"Think of what? What are you talking about?"

"Dee—one of the ghost hunters, an old friend of my Gran's. She comes here every year hoping to contact her dead husband."

"So? What's the problem?"

"Archie," Emma said. "Dee's husband was named *Archie.*"

Todd's mouth fell open. "So, if Viv thinks the ghost is Dee's husband . . ."

"She'll call Archie's name. And if Archie is trapped inside the walls . . ."

"He'll start barking to let us know where he is."

Emma looked at the door. "We've got to stop the séance."

"How? Everybody's already in there."

"I don't know," she said. "But we've got to try."

CHAPTER 23

The Spirit Room was packed when Todd and Emma walked in. Todd was surprised. This wasn't like the séances he'd seen on TV, with people sitting around a table while someone banged on it from underneath. The participants were on chairs arranged in two concentric circles, while sitting cross-legged in the middle was Viv Van Vandevander. A candle was burning on the floor in front of her. Its flame flickered as the door behind them closed.

"I'm going to go talk to Lars," Emma whispered. "Why don't you take a seat?"

"Shouldn't I stay here?" Todd said. "What if he says no?"

She shrugged helplessly and shook her head.

"Beats me," she said. "But believe me, it'll be harder with the two of us."

Todd glanced around the room and noticed with regret that the only empty seat was the one next to Gwen. Excusing himself as he hurried past, he crossed the room in front of the others and sat down.

"Sorry it took me so long," he whispered. "I was hoping we could call this thing off."

"Why?" Gwen said. "Are you afraid of ghosts now?"

"No, because I think the only ghost around here is Archie

and I'd rather not have a mob go after Emma if these people find out."

"What?"

As heads turned toward them, Todd put a finger to his lips.

"Dr. Richards said there were passages inside the walls," he whispered. "I think Archie might have gotten in there somehow."

"That stupid dog has ruined everything," Gwen muttered. "You should have just taken him to the pound."

Todd looked back to see if Emma was having any luck persuading Lars. As she whispered something in his ear, the professor shook his head vehemently. What were they going to do if he refused to call it off?

The question quickly became moot as Lars reached over and turned down the lights. The candle's flickering flame cast eerie shadows on the walls and turned the faces in the circle into ghoulish masks. On the floor in front of them, Viv closed her eyes and began to sway. There were whispers around the circle, and Todd was surprised when Gwen slipped her hand into his and squeezed it. He supposed he couldn't blame her. Even for someone who didn't believe in ghosts, it felt pretty eerie.

There was a thump overhead and someone in the audience squealed. Muted cries of, "Hush!" filled the room and then died down again. Todd looked for the noise's source but saw only shadows dancing overhead. It hadn't sounded like Archie, he thought. But if it wasn't Archie, what was it?

Viv appeared to have gone into some sort of trance. As she continued to sway, she filled the room with a low hum. At length, the humming stopped.

"Someone is here," she said.

The quality of Viv's voice had changed. To Todd, it sounded as if two people were speaking instead of one. He wasn't the only one in the room who'd noticed, either. People around him exchanged startled looks.

Lars called to her from his place by the door.

"Vivienne," he said, "why have they come?"

Viv moaned.

"To witness," she said. "To make amends. To ask for . . . forgiveness."

Todd heard a scuffle directly overhead and then an ear-piercing howl that sounded like Archie. Three people stood to leave and the others coaxed them back down. He searched the room, looking for Emma. Where was she? he wondered. Had she recognized it, too?

Lars continued his interrogation.

"Forgiveness?" he said. "For what?"

There was another howl and Viv jerked like a marionette. When she spoke again, her voice had deepened.

"I shouldn't have left you. I'm sorry."

Gwen gasped and grabbed his arm. Todd looked over and saw the woman on the other side of her struggling to stand.

"Archie?" she said in a tremulous voice. "Archie, is that you?"

Todd panicked. This must be Dee, he thought. The one Emma had warned him about. The one who'd come to every convention hoping in vain to contact her late husband, Archie. He had to stop her. If she called him again, Archie might hear her and start barking. If that happened, even the true believers in the room would realize they'd been had.

He leaned toward her.

"Excuse me, ma'am," he said. "Can I help you?"

Dee struggled to her feet. She was trembling; there were tears running down her cheeks.

"Oh, my darling, don't be sorry," she said. "It was my fault. I should have told you—"

Something heavy fell against the ceiling and Todd ducked as bits of plaster pelted the floor. He looked up and saw a crack race across the ceiling, widening as it went. He looked at Gwen.

"Get out of here! The whole thing is coming down!"

Gwen ran for the door as Dee clutched her chest and Todd rushed forward to catch her. There was a tremendous crash and people screamed, shoving their chairs aside as they ran headlong for the exit.

From her place beside the door, Emma watched in horror as chunks of plaster and lath tumbled down, followed by an enormous beam that hit the floor with a sound like cannon fire. Then, one by one, fifty-pound bags of rice and flour began falling through the hole, bursting open as they hit the ground and sending thick, powdery clouds into the air.

As people ran past her, choking and gasping for air, she saw Clifton drop from the hole in the ceiling. His green jacket looked like a snow-dusted fir and there was blood running down his face from a gash on his forehead. Under his left arm, Archie squirmed and growled, struggling to break free.

CHAPTER 24

Emma had set up a triage area in the banquet hall. As the steady stream of guests from the séance came through the door, she quickly directed them to the appropriate area for treatment. The inn had plenty of first aid supplies, including a defibrillator, plus blankets and cots for those who were too weak to stand or in danger of going into shock, and thanks to the SSSPA they also had two RNs, a naturopath, and a holistic healer on hand. Adam had earned high marks for remaining calm and dialing 911 when he heard the commotion, and the operator had assured him that the EMTs would be there soon.

Now, if I could just find Todd.

She wasn't particularly worried. In the mad scramble to evacuate the Spirit Room, people who weren't injured had fled to the safety of their hotel rooms. Emma had already seen Gwen retrieve Archie and whisk him away in his carrier; she figured Todd was probably back in his room getting ready to leave.

As much as Emma hated to see him go, she'd be glad to have Archie off the premises. The less the ghosts hunters saw of the little dog, the better the chances were that they wouldn't connect him to the encounters they'd been witnessing since the night before. With everything else that had gone wrong, the thought of losing her best customers was terrifying.

Though perhaps, Emma thought, not as terrifying as watching Clifton Fairholm fall through the ceiling. She glanced across the room at her assistant manager, sulking in the corner, who was waiting for the police to arrive while Dick Richards loomed over him like a white-haired vulture. The gash on Clifton's forehead had been bloody and he was badly bruised, but there was no sign that he'd suffered any serious injury.

Emma still had no idea what, exactly, he'd been doing up there, but the sight of all those supplies falling through the ceiling had made it pretty clear that he was at least partially responsible for the inn's precarious financial position. The thought that the man she'd trusted to guide her after Gran died had been doing his best to ruin her made Emma feel sick. There were anxious murmurs at the door and Lars Van Vandevander staggered into the room holding Viv in his arms.

"I need help here, stat!"

As a nurse rushed over, Viv reached up and brushed plaster dust from her hair.

"I told you I'm all right," she said. "Now, put me down, please."

Emma helped Lars get Viv onto a cot. There were cuts on her arms and a swelling on her collarbone that looked ominous. With all the plaster dust in her hair, she might have suffered a concussion, as well. Emma grabbed one of the thermal blankets and wrapped it around Viv's shoulders.

"Let him spoil you a little," she said. "It's a husband's prerogative."

As the nurse began checking his wife's wounds, Lars pulled Emma aside.

"I checked on Dee."

"How is she?"

"As well as can be expected," Lars said. "We've covered her with a blanket and I've got a couple of ladies sitting with her, but I'd rather not move her until the paramedics arrive."

"Good idea. Thank you."

Tears of relief sprang to Emma's eyes. The thought that they might lose Dee had weighed heavily on her mind.

Lars cleared his throat.

"However, I'm afraid the news isn't all good," he whispered. "There appears to be someone trapped underneath the rubble. If so, I'm afraid the ceiling fell right on top of them."

Emma gasped. "Are you sure?"

He nodded.

"Dee says she felt someone push her out of the way as the ceiling came down." Lars frowned. "You don't happen to know who was sitting beside her, do you?"

She did. Emma felt her throat constrict.

"It was Todd and his fiancée," she said. "But I know Gwen's all right. I saw her leave a few minutes ago."

"Was Todd with her?"

Emma shook her head and pressed a trembling hand to her mouth. Todd couldn't be under there, she thought. He just couldn't.

Lars leaned over and gently placed a hand on his wife's un-injured shoulder. The nurse had already bound the other arm to her side and was dabbing disinfectant on her forehead.

"Wait here a moment, will you, dear? I'll be right back."

Viv looked at him crossly. "What else can I do? I'm trussed up here like a turkey."

"That's my girl," he said, kissing the top of her head.

He glanced at Emma.

"You go ahead," he told her quietly. "I'll get some of the other men and join you in a minute."

Emma hurried out the door, trying to tamp down a growing sense of panic. Lars must have been exaggerating, she told herself. No one else had said anything about there being someone trapped in there. Besides, most of the people she'd been treating had only minor injuries. Even Dee, who'd been directly underneath the ceiling when it fell, was still alive. But as she stepped across the threshold, her heart sank.

The devastation was far worse than she'd realized. Now that the clouds of dust and flour had settled, the full extent of the damage was clearly visible. It looked like a bomb had gone off. There was broken plaster, shattered wood, and flour everywhere, some of it tinged with blood. Emma saw Dee lying amongst the wreckage, a thermal blanket draped over her, holding the hand of one of the women who sat with her. For just a moment, Emma felt relieved.

Then she saw Todd. His body was so deeply covered in debris that at first she'd mistaken him for one of the broken sacks of flour. He was on his stomach, arms outstretched, with one leg pinned beneath the heavy wooden beam. Emma began picking her way through the fragments of wood and plaster, her heart in her throat. She saw blood seeping from multiple wounds on Todd's head and hands and felt a surge of hope. That wouldn't happen if he were dead, she thought. Would it?

Lars and three other men appeared at the door.

"Did you find anyone?"

Emma nodded.

"It's Todd," she said, her voice so thick it almost choked her. "We need to get him out of here."

"Is he alive?" he said, as the four of them waded into the mess.

"I don't know. Let me check."

Emma got down on her hands and knees and reached for Todd's arm, gently encircling his wrist with her trembling fingers. *Please,* she thought. *Please.*

She felt a pulse—weak, but unmistakable.

"Yes," she said, as tears sprang to her eyes. "He's still alive."

There was a sudden rush of air in the room and Emma heard rapid, heavy footfalls coming down the hall.

"The EMTs are here," Lars said.

Todd's fingers moved and his eyelids fluttered.

"Oh, thank God," Emma said. "Thank God."

Gwen stood at the open door, watching Lars and the other men lift the heavy beam from Todd's leg. The EMTs had already started an IV and given him painkillers, but he'd refused to let Emma leave his side. The two of them were holding hands like a pair of newlyweds.

The other guests were darting pitying looks in Gwen's direction, and no one had congratulated her on her fiancé's survival. It must have been obvious to everyone that the ring Todd had given her meant nothing. When the worst had happened, it was Emma he wanted.

As Todd was lifted onto a stretcher, Gwen felt a wave of anger engulf her. She'd told her parents about their engagement, even sent a picture of the ring to her best friends. How dare he do this to her? She almost wished that Todd had died rather than humiliate her like this. At least then, people would have pitied her for the *right* reason. She could have put on a brave face, wearing the engagement ring as a reminder of her loss, and people would have admired her for being strong. The fact that she'd already lost Todd to Emma would have remained her little secret.

They had him strapped to the gurney now. As the EMTs started wheeling him out, Todd finally let go of Emma's hand. Gwen felt nothing but hatred as they wheeled him past. She'd left her parents' house and driven all that way just to be dumped. What was she supposed to do now, pack up Todd's clothes and tidy the room for him? And what about Archie? Todd had already refused to give him away. Did he really think Gwen was going to just pack up the little mutt and take him home?

Todd had humiliated and abandoned her, and what had he suffered? Nothing but a few scrapes and scratches. Gwen balled her hands into fists, wishing that there was some way to strike back at him, to hurt him as badly as he'd hurt her.

She paused, thinking about the little dog who was back in the room, lying quietly in his carrier. Maybe, Gwen thought, there was a way to hurt Todd after all.

CHAPTER 25

Emma gave her name at the nurse's station and signed in. The LPN at the desk had just started her shift, but the charge nurse recognized her and asked how things were going.

"I've got my staff looking after the hotel and most of the guests have checked out." She glanced at the double doors separating the waiting area from the patients' rooms. "I just thought I'd come by and see how he was doing."

"Of course."

The woman gave her a knowing smile and Emma looked away. This was the third time she'd come by the hospital since Todd had been admitted the night before. By now, everyone on his floor probably thought they were lovers. She might have tried to straighten them out, but Emma knew it wouldn't do any good. *People believe what they want to believe,* she told herself. *Might as well enjoy it while it lasts.*

"How's the arm?" the nurse said, pointing to the cast that covered Emma's left forearm from wrist to elbow.

"Not too bad." She flexed her fingers. "Doc said it was just a hairline fracture. I never would have known without the X-ray."

"Well, you know the drill."

She handed Emma a gown and waited for her to use the hand sanitizer before pushing the button that opened the double doors.

Todd's room was the fifth door on the right—a double with an empty second bed. As Emma walked down the hall, she tried not to stare into the other rooms, each one a tableau of sickness and misfortune. Hospital visitors tended to hug the walls, she'd noticed, looking awkward and uncertain, while the patients all looked pretty much the same. It was as if putting on one of those gowns stripped people of their uniqueness, the only difference between them being whether or not their eyes were open.

A nurse in green scrubs walked by and smiled at her. Emma stopped.

"Has he had any other visitors?"

"I don't think so."

The woman made a quick detour and checked the clipboard that hung from a hook outside his room.

"Nope," she said. "Looks like you're the only one."

Emma fumed. She could understand why Todd's mother wasn't there—even if she'd gotten the voice mail Emma had left on her phone, she was too far away to get there quickly—and Claire might not even know that anything had happened to her brother. But where was Gwen? She was his fiancée, after all, or at least she had been. Gwen was the one who should have been sitting next to Todd's hospital bed, not her.

I knew there was a reason I didn't like her.

As Emma stepped into the room, she caught a whiff of antiseptic. The lights had been dimmed and the TV was unplugged. In addition to a broken leg, facial lacerations, and a dislocated shoulder, Todd had suffered a mild concussion. There was no sign of permanent damage, but until his brain was fully healed, the doctor said he should have as little outside stimulation as possible.

The covers were tucked neatly across his chest and their gentle rise and fall was reassuring. Emma pulled up a chair and sat down. She didn't bother waking him. It was enough just to sit there quietly, knowing that Todd was all right. And after all the revelations of the last several hours, she needed time to just sit and think. There was still an awful lot of stuff she had to process.

Why?

It was the question she'd been asking herself since yesterday, and Emma still didn't have an answer. Why would the man who'd practically run the Spirit Inn for almost twenty years suddenly decide to destroy it? All this time, Emma had been blaming herself for the inn's problems while Clifton was doing everything he could to undermine her. If he'd physically stabbed her in the back, it couldn't have hurt any worse than it did. When she thought about how naive she'd been not to suspect him, it made her feel foolish.

Maybe I deserved this.

It wasn't just the supplies, either. When she started looking through everything that had fallen out of the ceiling, Emma had found a second set of books that showed he'd been embezzling from the inn for years. Even if she could get the bank to reconsider their repayment demand, she had nothing left to pay them with. The best she could hope for would be to sell the resort and move on.

"Hey, you."

Emma started. She hadn't noticed that Todd was awake. He'd probably been lying there, wondering why she kept showing up.

"How're you feeling?" she said.

"Like Chicken Little." He grimaced.

"I called your mother to tell her what happened, but I had to leave a message. If you give me Claire's number, I can call her, too."

He nodded. "Any more stuff turn up?"

Emma shrugged. He meant were there any more surprises in the rubble. She felt guilty for having told him as much as she had the last time she was there, but once they got started on the subject, the whole thing had just come tumbling out. She told him it served him right for being such a good listener.

"I found the blueprints for the hotel."

"And?"

"I'm not surprised Jake couldn't find a way into the attic," she said. "The entire structure is a façade."

"What do you mean 'a façade'?"

"Originally, there were three separate buildings on the property. When the outside shell was constructed, it left a series of passageways between them."

"Which would explain the hollow walls."

Emma nodded. "It's not unheard of. Even now, people sometimes reuse foundations. Whoever redid the inn just went a little overboard."

"It also explains the ghost encounters. Archie must have found a way in there. When he started howling and scratching to get out . . ."

"People at the inn heard it coming from inside the walls and assumed they were hearing ghosts."

"But if Archie could get in there, other animals could have, too. Maybe that's what gave your grandmother the idea that the place was haunted."

"Maybe." She made a face.

Todd lay back and rubbed a hand across his forehead.

"But why was Archie up in the attic? It couldn't have been easy for him to climb up there."

"I've been thinking about that," Emma said. "I think it was the rats."

He squinted at her. "Rats?"

"Clifton had been complaining about rats in the hotel for months, but no one else ever saw them. Turns out, they were attracted by all the supplies he'd stuffed into the attic; I found a few of them in the rubble. I'd been wondering why Clifton was always disappearing in the middle of the day. He must have been up there, clearing the dead rats out of the traps."

"And you think that that's what attracted Archie?"

Emma nodded.

"But surely someone else would have noticed if it smelled that bad."

"It wouldn't have had to be all that bad for Archie to notice; dogs' noses are a lot more sensitive than ours are. When Clifton realized that Archie had gotten into the passageway, he knew he had a problem. What if you went searching for your dog and discovered his secret?"

Todd's pillow had bunched up on one side. He reached up, trying to adjust it, and winced.

"Here," she said, "let me get that."

Emma stood and gently lifted his head as she moved the pillow back into place.

"Is that better?"

"Much." He smiled. "Thank you."

"Anyway," she continued. "Clifton must have gone up there just before the séance to try to catch him. He didn't realize that the extra weight of the supplies had further weakened the damaged ceiling and when he made a grab for Archie, it collapsed."

"So what'll you do now?"

She shrugged. "Sell it, I guess. One of the ski lodges next to me would probably love to have some extra space. Unless you've changed your mind about buying it."

He shook his head.

"Any idea why Fairholm would try to ruin you?"

"None," she said. "The biggest disagreement we ever had was whether or not the staff should wear ascots."

"Oh, well, that's your reason right there," he said. "Heck, I'd burn the place down before I'd wear one of those things."

Emma laughed. "No, he was the one who wanted to *keep* them."

"Too bad. Could have been grounds for an insanity defense."

She tried to laugh again, but it came out as a sob. Todd reached out and touched her hand.

"Sorry," he said. "I didn't mean to make light of it. It's just the way I am, I guess. Better to laugh than to cry, huh?"

She nodded and wiped away a tear.

"Can you stay a minute," he said, "or do you have to run?"

"I can stay a little longer, I guess."

Todd stared thoughtfully at the ceiling.

"I've been thinking about a new theme for the inn."

Emma grimaced. "That concussion must be worse than I thought. I don't have an inn anymore, remember? Or at least I won't by the end of the month."

He smiled. "Aren't you going to ask me what it is?"

"All right," she said. "What's your idea?"

"Pet friendly."

"That's the theme?"

"Yes. Instead of a haunted inn with lots of expensive Victorian doodads, why don't you close the Spirit Inn for repairs and open it again as a destination resort where people and their animals can come and enjoy a vacation together? Call it the Pet-Friendly Inn or something."

"What made you think of that?"

"On the way out to your place, Archie and I stopped at a place called the Dog Days Inn. It was a dump—not even a real hotel—and it was packed! If people will pay to stay in a smelly place like that just so they can have their pets with them, just imagine how happy they'd be to bring their pets to a really nice place."

She frowned thoughtfully. "I suppose it could work."

"Of course it could. And once I pay off your loan—"

Emma put up her hands. "I don't need your charity."

"Yes, you do. Look," he said, "I already know what your situation is, and unless I miss my guess, you know what mine is, too."

Emma looked away and shrugged.

"I'm serious. And I'm not talking about a gift; I'm talking about an investment. A pet-friendly inn will bring in more customers than your ghosts ever did. Which reminds me . . ."

Todd lifted his head and looked around.

"Where's Archie?"

CHAPTER 26

When the red Ferrari pulled into the humane society's parking lot, Jody Davis whistled. There might be plenty of rich folks in Puget Sound, but you didn't see a lot of Italian sports cars out in Gold Beach. The driver's door opened and a tall blond woman stepped out, removed a small dog carrier from the passenger's seat, and headed for the front door. Jody shook her head.

"Looks like somebody's bringing in a stray," she said to the other desk clerk.

"Hope they like bad news."

"Yeah, me too."

Jody braced herself for an argument. They weren't accepting any strays at the moment—the shelter was full—and the woman who was picking her way carefully through the puddles outside didn't look like the type who took no for an answer. She shook her head. Who wore high heels on a day like that?

The front door swung open with a whoosh and the woman staggered inside, dropping the carrier hard enough to make the little dog inside yip in protest. Jody pressed her lips together. She loved almost every kind of animal. People, not so much.

"Can I help you?"

"Yes," the woman said. "I want to get rid of this dog."

Jody glanced at the animal in the carrier.

"I'm sorry," she said. "We're not taking animals for adoption at the moment."

"Oh, I don't want him adopted," the woman said. "He needs to be destroyed."

That surprised her. People rarely brought an animal in specifically to be put down.

"Why?" Jody said. "What's wrong with him?"

"He bit me," the woman said.

A quick tug of her sleeve revealed a bloody bandage on her left forearm.

"I was just trying to pet him and he turned on me."

Jody stepped out from behind the counter and squatted down in front of the carrier. The dog inside was some sort of mixed breed. Small, but not small enough to be a toy. He wasn't wearing a collar, either, though it looked as if he had been recently.

"Hey there, fella."

The little dog blinked and turned his head away.

"Are his vaccines up-to-date?"

"Why? You don't think he could have rabies, do you?"

Jody was studying the little mutt. He looked healthy enough and he wasn't showing any sign of aggression. What would make a little guy like that bite someone?

"Doesn't look like it. You said you were just petting him and he hauled off and bit you?"

The blond woman pressed her lips together.

"Pretty much," she said. "The man who sold him to me said he was pretty high-strung, but he was so cute I couldn't resist. It's weird, too. I've always had good luck with Craigslist."

Jody made a face. Seemed like every other week they had someone come in who'd gotten a sick or vicious dog through an online ad. Why didn't they come down to the animal shelter instead? The humane society had plenty of healthy, adoptable dogs. She stood back up.

"You should always know an animal's history before you take it into your home," she said. "I don't suppose you could get the guy who sold him to you to take the dog back."

"I don't think so. I mean, I met him in a park and all I've got is his e-mail address."

Jody pursed her lips. It seemed a shame to put down an animal like that. She'd have bet her eyeteeth that the blond woman had done something to provoke him, but there was no way for her to check out her story and the shelter was obligated to destroy any animal deemed to be vicious. She reached behind the counter and took out a release form.

"Here," she said. "Fill this out while I put him in back."

She picked up the carrier and headed into the back room where the animals awaiting euthanasia were kept. Vic, the veterinary assistant, was setting up the injection table when Jody walked in. She opened the carrier and removed the little dog.

"Got another one for you," she said.

Vic looked over. "What's his problem?"

"Beats me," she said. "His owner says he bit her, but he looks pretty docile to me."

Jody set the little mutt in the cage and watched him curl up. Something about the situation didn't seem right. Would the previous owner have sold him if he knew where he'd end up? Maybe there was more to this story than she'd been told.

"You're not going to put him down right now, are you?"

"I can, if you want," he said. "But we usually do them all at five, when the doc gets here. Why?"

She shook her head.

"I just have a hunch," she said. "Just leave him where he is for now."

The blond woman was already getting back into her car when Jody returned. She'd left the form on the counter with a twenty-dollar bill on top. Jody ran outside.

"Wait a minute!" she yelled.

The woman looked at her irritably.

"The form's on the counter. I don't need a receipt for the donation."

"I know," Jody said. "But don't you want your carrier?"

"No, thanks," the woman said. "I won't be getting another dog anytime soon."

Todd listened as Gwen's phone kicked his call over to her voice-mail box. He pressed the disconnect button and lay back on the bed. This was the fourth time he'd called her in half an hour and he'd already left two messages; it didn't make any sense to leave another one.

Emma had stepped out to call the inn. She needed to see how Jake and Adam were and she'd promised to have them check to see if there were any messages. Todd set the phone down. Gwen's taking off like she had was giving him a bad feeling.

She wouldn't hurt Archie, would she?

Don't be ridiculous, he told himself. Gwen might be hurt and upset, but she wasn't a monster, and their broken "engagement" had nothing to do with Archie. If Todd had just put the ring back in his dresser instead of sticking it inside the suitcase, it never would have happened. Chances were good that Gwen had either driven home with Archie or taken him to Claire's.

Of course! Why hadn't he thought of that before? Claire's

house wasn't too far away. He'd give his sister a call and see if Gwen and Archie were there.

Todd looked down at his phone and saw that he'd missed a call. It must have come in when he was calling Gwen. He checked the number and smiled. It was from Claire, probably calling to let him know that Gwen and Archie had arrived safe and sound. Talk about a coincidence. He hit "call back" and waited. Emma walked in as it started to ring; he held up a finger for her to wait a minute.

"Hey, Claire, it's me."

"Todd? *What the hell is going on?*"

"What?"

"I just got off the phone with Ma. She's practically hysterical, thanks to you."

He felt his jaw tighten. "Sorry. The next time I stand under a ceiling, I'll try not to let it fall on me."

Claire's voice dropped several decibels.

"What ceiling? What are you talking about?"

"I'm in the hospital. Didn't Ma get Emma's message?"

"She didn't say anything about a message. What happened to Archie?"

"That's what I was calling you about. Aren't he and Gwen at your place?"

"*Gwen?* Why the hell would she be here?"

"I thought Archie was with her," he told his sister.

"Archie's at the pound," Claire said. "They called Ma and told her they're putting him down. How could you do that, Todd? I told you we'd take him."

"I didn't take him to the pound! I've been in the hospital since yesterday."

"Well, *somebody* took him down there."

Todd finally noticed the look on Emma's face and realized she must have known something was wrong before she walked in.

"Hang on a second, Claire." He put his hand over the phone. "Do you know what's going on?"

She nodded. "A little. Your mother called the inn and said to tell you that you have to get Archie from the humane society by five or they'll put him to sleep."

"*What?* They can't do that." He uncovered the phone. "This has to be a mistake. How did the humane society get Ma's number?"

"Archie's chip. When they scanned it, they got Uncle Bertie's phone number and when they called it, they got forwarded to her."

"But the humane society doesn't put dogs down," he said.

"They do if they're vicious."

"Archie isn't vicious!"

"The woman who dropped him off said he was. Ma said she told them he'd bitten her."

Todd's head began to pound. It had to be Gwen; Emma had seen her put Archie in his carrier. But why would she do that? Why hurt Archie because she was angry with him?

It didn't matter. The important thing now was to get him out of there before the place closed.

"Can you go pick him up?" he asked.

"No, that's why I called you. Bob's taken the truck and I've got no way to reach him."

There was no other way. Todd would just have to get Archie himself.

"Which humane society was it, do you know?"

"Ma just said it had a three-sixty area code."

Which meant it could be anywhere. He looked at the clock. There wasn't time to call around and find the right one.

"Call Ma back. Tell her to check her caller ID for the number," he told his sister. "Then call me back."

"Okay, and then what?"

"Tell her not to worry. Tell her you talked to me and I'm going to get Archie."

Emma was shaking her head. Todd scowled at her and pointed to the clock.

"I thought you said you were in the hospital," Claire said.

"I was"—he reached under his gown and ripped the electrodes off his chest—"but I just checked out."

Todd knew that waiting for a doctor to sign him out was the preferred method for checking out of a hospital, but putting on his clothes and using the service elevator worked just as well. Emma pulled her truck up to the curb and helped him into the front seat.

"Where are we going?" he said.

"Gold Bar. The woman on the phone said you'll need to show ID and sign an affidavit swearing that Archie was stolen and that he hasn't bitten anyone. Do you need help?"

"Not anymore," Todd said, pulling his leg into the cab.

He slammed the door and Emma pulled away from the curb.

"How long does it take to get there?" he asked.

"Depends on what condition the roads are in. Twenty-five minutes if they're clear; twice that if there's ice on the road."

Todd checked the time. It was four twenty-seven.

"That's cutting it pretty close."

"I know," she said. "I'll do my best."

The truck's engine roared as they pulled out into traffic. They were on the highway in less than a minute, heading east toward Gold Bar.

"Thanks for taking me. I don't know how I'd have gotten to him, otherwise."

Emma looked over and smiled.

"It's okay. You'd have done the same for me."

Todd shook his head sadly. "This is my fault. If they put Archie down, I'll never forgive myself."

"How is it your fault? You didn't take him down there."

"No, but I didn't do anything to stop her, either."

"Um, excuse me? You were unconscious, remember?"

Todd licked his lips. How could he explain to her the person he'd become these last few years? To Emma, he was just a grown-up version of the little kid who'd done cannonballs off the diving board and shinnied up trees to spy into birds' nests. How could he make her understand that losing his father had undercut his sense of security, made him so desperate for outside validation and approval that he'd been willing to throw away his moral compass in favor of money in the bank and marriage to a beautiful woman who treated him badly?

"By the way, I like your idea," she said.

"What?"

"For the inn, remember? You know, somewhere people could go and stay with their animals where there'd be stuff for everyone to do. I'm still not sure about letting you—oh, no!"

Taillights were bunching up on the road in front of them. Emma took her foot off the gas.

"Looks like there's a wreck up there," she said as the truck slowed.

Todd took out his phone and checked the local traffic.

"It's on the right, just before the next exit."

"How much time have we got?"

"Eight minutes." He slammed his fist against the door. "Damn it!"

Emma put on her signal and started cutting over to the left-hand lane.

"Don't worry," she said. "We can still make it."

"How? There's no way this is going to clear in time."

"It doesn't have to." She pulled out onto the shoulder and gunned the engine. "But you'd better hold on."

CHAPTER 27

Outside the humane society, the truck screeched to a halt. As Todd struggled out of his seat, Emma jumped down and ran for the door. She grabbed the handle and pulled.

"It's locked!"

"It can't be," he said. "It's only four fifty-eight."

Todd tried the handle of the glass door, sending the bell on the other side clanging. He banged on the door with his fist.

"Open up! I'm here to get my dog!"

Emma ran back to the truck and laid on the horn.

"Come on!" Todd yelled. "Open up the damned door!"

A woman appeared behind the counter and hurried over.

"Hold on to your britches," she said, turning the lock. "What's this all about? We're closed."

The cast on Todd's leg was ungainly. As the door swung open he teetered, nearly losing his balance.

"You've got my dog," he said. "My mother got a call. I'm here to get him."

"Are you Archie's owner?"

"Yes, yes," Todd said, looking around. "Where is he?"

"Oh, dear," the woman said, glancing behind her. "I think they just put him down."

★ ★ ★

"Last one," Vic said as he reached into Archie's cage. "Come on, fella."

The vet glanced up at the clock. It had been a long day at the clinic. He was tired and ready to go home; he wasn't going to quibble over forty-five seconds. He picked up the syringe.

"Let's get this over with."

Vic laid Archie on his side and stroked him gently. It was too bad the little guy's owner hadn't shown up, he thought. Jody would be upset. People did that sometimes, said they were coming and then didn't bother. He wished they wouldn't do that.

The vet paused. "Do you hear something?"

They heard the sound of rushing footsteps and the door burst open.

"Stop!" Jody yelled. "Don't do it!"

A man with a cast on his leg hobbled into the room. He had one arm in a sling and the other around the neck of a petite brunette. His face was bruised and his head bandaged. Vic thought the guy looked like he'd been in a car wreck.

"Archie," the man sobbed. "You're alive!"

Vic released him and the little dog struggled to his feet.

Archie jumped into Emma's arms and she and Todd laughed as he licked their faces, his whole body wiggling with joy. Todd steadied himself against the table and carefully wrapped his arms around them both. This was what life was all about: love and family; someone to protect; someone to cherish and care for. He closed his eyes and a tear ran down his cheek. For the first time since his father had died, Todd felt whole.

"Let's get you out of here," he said. "You're coming home with us." He glanced at Emma. "*Both* of us."

EPILOGUE

Archie stood in the bathtub and tried not to shiver as he waited for Todd's mother to return with a towel. The bathwater tickled as it ran down behind his ears and along his back, but he resisted the urge to shake it off—a good dog didn't shake himself inside the house. When Fran returned, she rubbed him down with a towel, then placed him on the counter and used a hair dryer to finish the job. It was good to be dry and warm again. Archie wagged his tail to show his appreciation.

There was a box on the counter. Fran opened it and took out a small bundle wrapped in tissue paper. Inside it was a tiny black jacket with a built-in dress shirt and cummerbund.

"I found this when I was going through Bertie's things."

Excitement shot through him as she took Archie's front paws one at a time and pushed them through the sleeves. Fran clipped a bow tie to his collar and smoothed the fur back from his eyes.

"There, now," she said, setting him down on the floor. "You look like a proper gentlemen."

She took out her lipstick and drew a line of red across her mouth.

"Come along, we mustn't be late. Those two have waited long enough for this day."

Archie followed her to the front door and watched her pin her hat in place. Fran set her hand on the doorknob and gave him a stern look.

"Now, don't forget," she said. "You're not the star of this show. I expect you to behave."

Todd checked his watch. "What's taking so long? Ma said they'd be here by now."

"Don't fret, *dearthái̇r*," Claire said, fussing with the nosegay on his lapel. "No one likes an impatient bridegroom."

He frowned and fussed with his tie. Claire had been on her best behavior for months. The suspense was killing him.

"Go on," he said. "Say it. I know you want to."

His sister's face was all innocence. "Say what?"

"I told you so."

"Why ever would I do that?" She laughed. "You've already said it for me."

Emma stood in front of the mirror, smiling at her reflection. The simple linen shift had been her grandmother's; a wedding dress made for a war bride, given to her by the friend who promised to pass it along when the day came. Now it had been cleaned and altered to fit her. It was perfect.

"It's beautiful," she said. "Thank you."

Dee sat behind her, one hand on the cane that was now her constant companion.

"You're beautiful," she said. "A beautiful bride."

Emma swallowed the lump in her throat. With Gran and her mother both gone, she thought she'd have no one—no woman—to help her prepare for her wedding day. But when she told Dee she was getting married, she came at once. That she had brought Gran's wedding dress with her made Emma feel twice blessed.

Dee picked up the garland of wildflowers and set it on Emma's head, then handed her the bouquet.

"I think it's time now, don't you?"

Emma took Jake's arm and he walked her down the aisle, past the folding chairs they'd set up in the lobby. Todd stood with the minister by the front desk, beaming as his bride approached. Jake gave him a stern look before releasing Emma's hand and taking his seat.

Archie was the ring bearer and he took his job seriously. In his pint-sized tux, and with a satin pillow strapped to his back, he waited until the rings were requested, then stepped forward and patiently waited while they were untied. When that was done, he sat back and watched as his two favorite people exchanged vows in front of God and their witnesses.

And when at last the minister pronounced Todd and Emma man and wife, Archie kissed the bride.

Keep reading for some special advice from the creators of GoPetFriendly.com on how to take your furry friend on the vacation of a lifetime!

PREPARING FOR YOUR
FIRST DOG-FRIENDLY VACATION

By Amy Burkert, Pet Travel Expert at
GoPetFriendly.com

You've been dreaming about it for years, and it's finally happened. . . . For the first time in your life, you have your very own dog! Of course, he's perfect in every way. You've already taught him some basic commands, and now you're ready to strike out on your first big adventure together. You can almost see the miles of open road, feel the wind in your hair, and imagine all the new scents along the way. It's going to be perfect, but first you'll have to do a little preparation to be sure your first dog-friendly vacation comes off without a hitch!

A road trip is the best kind of vacation with your dog. It allows you to set your own pace and decide moment by moment what sounds like fun. Laying out your route and locating accommodations and activities along the way is easy when you use a pet-friendly road-trip planner, but there are a few other things you'll need to think about before you take off!

Prepare Your Vehicle

In addition to making sure your car is tuned up for your trip, you'll need to get it "pet ready" before you hit the road.

Making sure you come home together safely is the most important part of any trip, so be sure you have a way of securing your pet while you are traveling.

Crates, carriers, or car harnesses will prevent your dog from making an unannounced visit to check the view from your lap while you're driving and will protect him from injury in case of an accident. Also remember to deactivate the airbag for any seat your pet will be occupying.

Talk to Your Vet

Call your vet to confirm that your dog's vaccinations are up to date, and discuss any possible health concerns that might exist where you will be traveling. Also ask about possible remedies for car sickness, diarrhea, and restlessness—just in case!

Finally, consider having your pet microchipped and keep your contact information up to date with the company that registers the chip. It would be a nightmare, but pets do become separated from their people while traveling. Shelters, animal hospitals, veterinary clinics, and humane societies have scanners that read the chips so they can quickly notify you of your pet's recovery.

Polish Your P's and Q's

You can avoid embarrassing and potentially dangerous situations by teaching your dog reliable come, heel, quiet, and settle commands. Practice is the key. Before you set out, test your progress somewhere with a lot of distractions, like an outdoor café or a dog park.

Gather the Gear

Dogs need a lot of stuff when they are on vacation! Here's a checklist of things you'll want to take along:

- Food and treats—If you are not certain that you'll be able to find the brand of food and treats you feed your pet along the way, pack enough for the whole trip plus a little extra. And, for canned food, don't forget the can opener!

- All his medications, vitamins, and supplements.

- Drinking water—If your dog's stomach is easily upset, it pays to take drinking water from home with you.

- Food and water bowls—Portable bowls pack easily and are great when you are out and about, and anti-spill water bowls are fantastic in the car.

- Your dog's bed and a couple of toys—These familiar objects will make him more comfortable when you spend the night in unfamiliar locations.

- Current identification tag—Of course you'll want to include your cell phone number, or other phone number where you can be reached while you are away, on your dog's ID tag. If your dog requires medication, include that information on his tag as well.

- Leash—Many places require your pet to be on a leash no longer than six feet. Also consider a long leash (fifteen to twenty feet) if you plan to hike with your dog or let him run in an unfenced area.

- Waste bags to pick up after him along the way.

- A couple of rolls of paper towels and some carpet cleaner for muddy paws and other messes.

- An old towel in case of rain, or after swimming.

- First aid kit.

- Proof of vaccinations—You'll need these at some dog parks, hotels, and campgrounds. Also, if you need to use a pet sitter, day care, or kennel services while you are traveling, they will need these documents.

- Medical records—Having your pet's veterinary records with you could be critical in the event of an injury or illness. Rather than lugging around a large file, scan the documents to an easy-to-pack USB drive. And don't forget to take your vet's telephone number and the telephone number for the ASPCA Animal Poison Control Center: 888-426-4435.

- Photo of your dog—In case you get separated, have a current photo handy so you can create posters quickly.

All this preparation takes some time, but it's the secret to making sure your trip is enjoyable for everyone. With the groundwork done, it's time to decide where you'll go and what you'll see!

Less Is More When It Comes to Fun

Start poking around and you'll find that there are thousands of places that would be fun to visit with your dog. From hiking in the mountains to romping on the beach, the possibilities are almost endless! It's tempting to jam-pack your itinerary with all of the pet-friendly locations you'll find along the way, but remember to leave time to stop and sniff the roses.

To a dog, nothing is more important than thoroughly sniffing the tree before him. Rushing him on to the next tree, and the one after that, before he's finished with the first is just plain frustrating. When you're traveling with your pet, plan to take your time. Trade in your scurry for a mosey, and really experience the places you go rather than just checking them off a list.

Booking a Place to Stay

Reserving a pet-friendly hotel can be a tricky proposition. While more and more locations welcome pets, the degree of enthusiasm with which your dog will be received ranges from "barely pet tolerant" to "over-the-top accommodating." Ask these questions, and you'll have all the information you need to find the perfect place to stay:

Does the hotel accept pets? Hotel pet polices change often, so it's a good idea to verify that the property you're considering is still welcoming pets.

Are there any weight or breed restrictions? It's common for hotels to impose weight restrictions—but if you've found a hotel that's perfect in every way, except that your pup is a little too big, ask if they'll make an exception! Most hotels have a little wiggle room in their size limitations and will try to accommodate you when asked.

How many pets are allowed per room? When you travel with multiple pets, it's important to ask if you'll all be allowed to stay in the same room together.

Will you be charged additional pet fees? This is where a

hotel's true pet-friendly colors will show. There are some hotel chains where pets stay free, while others heap on pet fees that can add up to more than the nightly room rate! Be sure you have a clear understanding of the charges before making your reservation. Determine whether the fee is per night or for the entire stay, whether it's charged per pet or is a fixed rate regardless of the number of pets, and whether any portion of the fee is refundable if the room isn't damaged during your stay.

Are pet travelers limited to specific pet-friendly rooms? Everyone has their preferences . . . proximity to the elevator, stairwell, ice machine, and high floors versus low floors. It's good to know up front if the hotel will accommodate your requests.

What amenities does the hotel offer? The most important amenity is always a convenient, grassy pet relief area, but some hotels also provide treats at check-in, pet beds and bowls in the room, doggy room service menus, spa treatments, and pet-sitting services. Some hotels have restaurants with pet-friendly patios, and some even host a "yappy hour" in the lobby each evening! Deciding how much to pamper your pooch is up to you.

May pets be left unattended in the room? Determining whether the hotel allows you to leave your pet alone in the room while you step out for something to eat or to run an errand helps you plan appropriately. Hotels are primarily concerned with two things when dogs are left unattended: damage to the room and barking that disturbs other guests. To alleviate those concerns, the hotel may require that pets be crated when you're away, and following our tips for a quiet stay will help ease any worries with barking.

Are some areas of the hotel off-limits to pets? Pets are generally not allowed in breakfast areas, restaurants, pools, and fitness rooms, so ask to be sure you can live with the restrictions.

Is the hotel haunted? It's best to know up front if there's a chance you and your dog will be sharing your room with a ghost. If in fact you find yourselves lodging with Casper the Friendly Poltergeist, ask for another room.

Keep to the Schedule

Maintaining your dog's feeding and exercise schedule as much as possible during your trip will reduce any anxiety he may feel about being away from home. Set an alarm to remind you when mealtime is approaching, and set aside time each day to let your dog stretch, run, and burn off some energy—isn't this what being on vacation is all about, after all?

Be Considerate

When you travel with your pet, you are an ambassador for all pet travelers—so make a good impression! Abide by the rules of the places you visit—especially keeping your dog on-leash and always cleaning up after him. Inconsiderate behavior can have unfortunate repercussions for future pet travelers and local pet owners.

Roll with It

When things go a little sideways—and they sometimes will—you can choose to let it ruin your day, or you can choose to see it as a new adventure. Dogs are great teachers in that they're never attached to the outcome . . . where you end up, how many places you see along the way. . . . Those things are all irrelevant to your dog. He just wants to be with you and have fun. If you can embrace that mind-set, you'll see every detour as an opportunity to have a great time—and you and your dog will grow closer for the experience.

With these tips in hand, your first dog-friendly vacation will be a breeze! And, most important, you'll be making memories with your best friend that will last a lifetime.

About GoPetFriendly.com

In 2009 two accountants returned from walking their dog, Ty, and found a stray German shepherd waiting on their doorstep. They took the poor dog inside and mounted a search for his people, but no one came forward to claim him. So they named him Buster and made him part of their family . . . and that changed everything.

It wasn't long until the couple was planning their summer vacation and discovered how difficult it was to travel with a dog as big as Buster! Hotels had weight restrictions and some charged ridiculous pet fees, and information on pet-friendly restaurants, beaches, and dog parks was scattered all over the Internet. That's when Amy and Rod Burkert came up with the idea to start a Web site that would make it easy to plan trips the whole family could enjoy together.

Now GoPetFriendly.com has it all. From pet-friendly hotels and campgrounds to beaches and off-leash parks where your dog can run—even veterinarians, pet supply stores, restaurants, and wineries—you'll get the scoop on more than 60,000 pet-friendly locations across North America!

All the information pet parents need when traveling in the United States and Canada is provided free of charge, including 20,000 consistent, detailed pet policies from hotels and campgrounds, expert advice on nearly 200 dog-friendly destination guides, and a pet-friendly road-trip planner that makes planning your next vacation a breeze.

Amy, Rod, Ty, and Buster have been touring the country in their motor home for more than five years, searching out new pet-friendly places to include on the Web site, and blogging about their adventures. They invite you to travel vicariously with them on the GoPetFriendly.com blog, Take Paws, and on Facebook, Instagram, Pinterest, and Twitter.

Waggin' trails!